Praise for the authors of

WHAT LIES BENEATH

"Anne Stuart is...one of the most
electrifying voices in suspense today."
—*Romantic Times*

"There are very few authors who write
to the level of excellence displayed by Ms. Stuart.
She takes intrigue, adventure and excitement,
adds a hot romance...and the result is pure joy."
—*Romantic Times*

"With great storytelling, excitement and energy,
Joanna Wayne shines..."
—*Romantic Times*

"Ms. Burnes delivers a complicated mystery
destined to thrill readers..."
—*Romantic Times*

Anne Stuart has written over sixty novels in her more than twenty-five years as a writer. She has won every major award in the business, including three RITA® Awards from Romance Writers of America, as well as their Lifetime Achievement Award. Anne's books continue to make national and chain bestseller lists, and she has been quoted in *People, USA TODAY* and *Vogue.* When she's not writing or traveling around the country speaking to various writers' groups, she can be found at home in northern Vermont with her husband and two children.

Joanna Wayne lives with her husband just a few miles from steamy, exciting New Orleans, but her home is the perfect writer's hideaway. A lazy bayou, complete with graceful herons, colorful wood ducks and an occasional alligator, winds just below her back garden. When not creating tales of spine-tingling suspense and heartwarming romance, she enjoys reading, traveling, playing golf and spending time with family and friends. Joanna believes that one of the special joys of writing is knowing that her stories have brought enjoyment to or somehow touched the lives of her readers.

Caroline Burnes continues her life as doorman and can opener for her six cats and three dogs. E. A. Poe, the prototype cat for Familiar, rules as king of the ranch, followed by his lieutenants, Miss Vesta, Gumbo, Chester, Maggie the Cat and Ash. The dogs, though a more lowly life form, are tolerated as foot soldiers by the cats. They are Sweetie Pie, Maybelline and Corky.

ANNE STUART
JOANNA WAYNE
CAROLINE BURNES

WHAT LIES
BENEATH

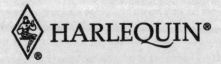

HARLEQUIN®

TORONTO • NEW YORK • LONDON
AMSTERDAM • PARIS • SYDNEY • HAMBURG
STOCKHOLM • ATHENS • TOKYO • MILAN • MADRID
PRAGUE • WARSAW • BUDAPEST • AUCKLAND

ISBN 0-373-83531-0

WHAT LIES BENEATH

CONTENTS

THE ROAD TO HIDDEN HARBOR   9
Anne Stuart

REMEMBER ME   133
Joanna Wayne

PRIMAL FEAR   257
Caroline Burnes

THE ROAD TO
HIDDEN HARBOR

Anne Stuart

CHAPTER ONE

MOLLY FERRELL pulled her car to a stop on the bluff overlooking the ocean, switching off the engine and putting the stick shift in first gear. She'd been sitting in her cramped little Honda for the better part of two days, and she was finally within sight of her destination. Hidden Harbor, Maine, was a small town halfway up the seacoast, nestled between two spits of land, and even in the bustling new millennium it still remained relatively secluded.

Of course, it wasn't high summer. Autumn had come, turning the leaves to shades of gold and brass and copper, the summer vacationers had departed, and most of the inns and bed-and-breakfasts had closed for the season. She'd been lucky to find a place to stay. There was always the larger town of Sanford some thirty miles away, but that wouldn't have been half as effective. She needed to live in Hidden Harbor itself. To find the answers she needed.

She'd had to make her reservation the old-fashioned way, by telephone, since the Internet had proven surprisingly unhelpful. Just when she was ready to give in and call the Sanford Holiday Inn, her luck had changed. The Harbor Inn was closed for repair and renovations, but the owner, Marjorie Twitchell, could offer her a room and not much else if she was willing to rough it.

Molly would have pitched a tent on the town green if she had to. She'd managed to finagle three months leave to finish her research. By January she'd be back teaching at the huge educational factory that was Southern Michigan University, and she was going to have to work fast if she was at least going to have a decent outline for her book under her belt. Though deep in her heart of hearts she was hoping for a rough draft.

It was time to get on with her life. Time to put away childish things. Her near obsession for a long-dead writer was just that—a remnant from her dreamy-eyed adolescence. If she ever wanted to make tenure then she had to let go of the ghost of Michael O'Flannery. And she'd come to Hidden Harbor to do just that.

Why couldn't she have had a crush on someone normal, like an actor or a rock star instead of a relatively obscure poet? Michael O'Flannery had lived and died shrouded in mystery, and only the barest details had surfaced, most of them suspect. In the twenty years since he'd killed himself he'd been almost forgotten. One brilliant novel and a collection of gorgeous, morbid poetry could only carry a reputation so far. His mysterious death added to the allure, as had his youth, but even that had faded in the past few years, making O'Flannery nothing more than a literary footnote. And leaving a strange, impractical obsession that had started when she was an impressionable fifteen-year-old and still haunted her more than a decade later. She loved his words and his images, the quirky way his mind had worked. She loved everything about him, including his tragic fate.

If she could find the truth then maybe she could let go of him. Tear his short, brilliant life into little pieces to be examined and prodded and then packed away.

She was ready to move on, ready to turn past lost poets, past broken engagements, past dreamy vulnerability into hardheaded practicality.

It was time she grew up. Once she made tenure she wouldn't want to leave the university. Wouldn't dare to leave that kind of security. If she was going to have choices in her life she needed to do something about it now, before it was too late.

The town of Hidden Harbor looked peaceful from her vantage point. There were no fancy yachts moored in the harbor—only sturdy fishing boats. Lobster boats most likely. She knew from her research that lobstering was the major industry in the small town. Those who didn't work in the trade were pretty much destitute. Like Michael O'Flannery's drunken father.

None of his family had survived him—he'd had no siblings, no aunts or uncles, and his parents had died in a car accident before he'd killed himself. But there'd be neighbors. People who'd been there when he'd grown up, who'd have stories, memories. Who might know something that would lead to the truth about Michael O'Flannery. What demons had

driven him to write such dark, haunted prose?
And what had driven him to take a gun and
walk into the woods, never to be seen again?

If she were really lucky she might even find
a photograph of him. He'd been notoriously
camera shy during his short time in the spot-
light, and the only pictures that remained were
shots of the back of his head. She'd spent years
of her life fantasizing about someone and she
didn't even know what he looked like.

In a way, that had been part of his appeal.
He could be anything she wanted—tall, short,
lean, muscle-bound, close-cropped dark hair or
long blond curls. It was one more way she was
able to convince herself she was in love with
his words, not the man himself. How could you
love someone you'd never even seen?

She took a deep breath, the tang of the salt
sea air in her lungs. It had been years since
she'd even seen the ocean. She'd forgotten
how oddly soothing it was, to sit and watch the
waves batter against the rocks. Lake Michigan,
vast and beautiful as it was, just didn't cut it.

She'd grown up in a small, coastal town on
Rhode Island, right on the water, and she
would have thought she'd had enough of the

ocean's vast changeability. She'd forgotten how it got in your veins and stayed there. She looked down at the quiet fishing village. She'd never been there in her life, and yet it felt like home. The ocean called to her, almost as strongly as Michael O'Flannery's legend, and she realized for the first time she wanted to come back. To live by the sea again. It wasn't going to be any time soon. She couldn't afford oceanfront property any more than she could abandon teaching. But this would be a taste of it, enough to tide her over for a few years.

She climbed back in her car, shoving her hair away from her face. "I'm going to find you, Michael O'Flannery," she murmured. "I'm going to find your ghost and everything I can about you. Just watch me."

There was no answer on the sharp ocean breeze. But then, she hadn't expected one. She turned the key, put the car in gear and started down the winding road to Hidden Harbor.

It was easy enough to find the Harbor Inn. There wasn't much to the town—people probably drove over to nearby Sanford for shopping or movies. Half the houses were shuttered and closed up against the coming winter, and even though the weather was still relatively warm there was a cold, dark feeling to the place.

She was being melodramatic, a weakness of hers, Molly thought. It was nothing more than a seaside community reacting to the economic realities of the changing seasons. A bit smaller than usual, a bit more behind the times. The place probably hadn't changed much in the last thirty years, unlike the rest of the seacoast. Maybe not in the last fifty years.

Which would suit her just fine. The town would have looked the same when Michael O'Flannery was growing up. She would finally begin to know what his life had actually been like.

It was late afternoon, and the shadows on the empty streets were long and somber. The Harbor Inn was at one end of the town, overlooking the harbor and the vast Atlantic beyond it. It was a large, rambling building, in dire need of paint and a new roof. She could hear the muffled sounds of hammers and power tools as she pulled up in the empty parking lot, and she winced. Marjorie Twitchell had warned her there'd be noise and dust, but

Molly hadn't really had any choice in the matter. Besides, the inn was more than a hundred years old. O'Flannery himself must have been inside that building during his short lifetime. She'd actually be under the same roof where he may have once been. Breathe the same air, walk the same floors. The thought was disturbingly exciting.

So she was a little obsessed. What was the problem with that? It was good to get involved in your work, wasn't it? O'Flannery was simply a fascinating character study. Anyone would be caught up in the legend and drama. Her former fiancé had once told her in a jealous fit that she was in love with O'Flannery. Well, maybe she was, just a little bit. He was long dead—what harm would a little fantasy do her? Except that Robert always insisted that as long as she loved O'Flannery she'd never love him.

Well, she had more reason than ever to love her lost poet. Robert was a jerk, and she was well rid of him. It was her pride that was hurt, not her heart. Which for some reason made it even worse.

She hauled her suitcase and laptop out of the

car and headed for the front door. It was thick, solid wood, and she doubted her knocking would carry very far over the sounds of carpentry. There was no bell, but after a moment she tried the polished brass doorknob. It wasn't locked.

She stepped into the hall, dumping her luggage on the faded Oriental carpet, and caught her breath. It was like stepping into another century. Dust motes danced in the air, and she could smell the years mixing with the tang of the ocean and the sweet scent of fresh lumber. If anyone could bottle that fragrance they'd make a fortune, Molly thought. When she made her way back to Michigan she'd only have the memory of that evocative smell.

"Hello?" she called into the rambling old house. Her voice probably didn't penetrate much farther than her knocking had. She closed the door behind her, shutting the world outside, and headed in the direction of the noise.

She found the source of the voices easily enough in the torn-apart kitchen. She pushed open a door and the sudden silence was shocking.

"You must be Dr. Ferrell!" A plump, middle-aged woman stepped forward, a nervous smile on her face. "Welcome to Hidden Harbor! I'm sorry I didn't hear you knock— Jake and Davy have been making a terrible racket. I'm Marjorie Twitchell, of course, and these two are my carpenters, Jake and Davy. Jake, this is Molly Ferrell. Remember, I told you she'd be staying here for the next few weeks?"

"You told me," the man said. "You just neglected to tell me why until five minutes ago."

He turned and looked at her, and the hostility in his dark blue eyes was startling. She'd never seen the man in her life, but he'd already decided he didn't like her.

"Now, Jake..." Mrs. Twitchell began in a plaintive voice.

But Jake wasn't listening to her—he was concentrating the full force of his attention on Molly. He was good-looking, maybe ten years older than she was, with long dark hair and cold eyes and good bones. Not that she was interested—she'd sworn off everyone but Michael O'Flannery for the next three months.

And clearly this man was even less impressed with her.

"She's here to dig up old bones and to poke her nose where it doesn't belong." He had a deep, implacable voice, one that sent an odd little shiver down her spine.

"I'm not here to do any such thing," she protested. "Michael O'Flannery was a wonderful writer, and I don't want his work lost and forgotten."

Jake simply looked at her for a long moment. It made her nervous. "Maybe he's better off forgotten. Let him rest in peace."

"I can't," she said simply.

"What's she talking about, Jake?" She hadn't seen the other man standing in the shadows, which was astonishing, since he was huge, even taller than Jake, massive and hulking. He was looking at her out of wide, child-like eyes, and he moved into the light with a shambling gait, a mix of curiosity and hostility etched on his face.

"Nothing, Davy," Jake said in a calm voice. "She's just another tourist."

"The tourists are gone. What's she got to do

with Michael? Is she going to bring him back?''

"Michael's not coming back, Davy. He's been dead and gone for twenty years, remember?''

"I remember," Davy said. He took another step toward her. "She's pretty.''

"Davy!" Jake's deep voice held a warning, but Davy wasn't listening. He moved across the kitchen, coming straight toward her. "She's pretty, Jake," he said in his singsong voice. "I don't think we need to worry.''

It was enough to make Jake move. He crossed the room and took Davy's arm, pulling him away from her with surprisingly gentle hands.

"There's nothing to worry about anyway, Davy," he said patiently. "I'll take you home now.''

"But we have more work to do.''

"We can wait until after she's gone.''

"I'm not going to be in anyone's way," Molly said. Jake's blue eyes slid over her, and she controlled her nervous start. "I'll be out talking to people, doing research...''

"You're wasting your time here," he said.

"Marjorie should have told you that. You should never have come here in the first place."

"I beg your pardon?" she said, trying to summon her frostiest voice.

He was cold enough to begin with. "You heard me," he said. "No one's going to tell you a damned thing. Come on, Davy."

And the door slammed shut behind him.

"Oh, my," Mrs. Twitchell said. "He has such a temper. I should have warned you Jake might be a bit difficult. Just pay him no mind, dear. He'll get over it."

"What's his problem?"

"The same problem you'll encounter wherever you go," she said in her cheerful little voice. "Michael O'Flannery."

IT COULD have been worse, Jake thought, once he dropped Davy off at his parents' house. There'd been other academics over the years, showing up in Hidden Harbor, asking questions, prying through things. Molly Ferrell was younger than most, and she didn't have that hard-edged, professional quality to her. As a matter of fact, she didn't look like a professor at all, though Marjorie Twitchell had assured him she was.

She was young—maybe late twenties. No more than ten years younger than he was, but a generation apart. She was pretty, too, in a soft, unspectacular way. Unfortunately he'd always been a sucker for warm brown eyes and long brown hair. And he couldn't help noticing her mouth.

He shook his head. He knew better than to let a pair of beautiful eyes distract him. So she was pretty. He was a healthy male who'd been surrounded by the same women for too long. It was only natural that he'd be…distracted by her.

But that was only a temporary reaction. She was trouble, despite her quiet voice and almost shy demeanor. She was here to poke her nose into places it didn't belong, and he needed to get rid of her, just as he'd gotten rid of the others over the years.

He didn't want to do it, but he would. Some things were just too precious to risk. The truth being one of them.

CHAPTER TWO

THE BREEZE had picked up, scudding the dry leaves down the empty sidewalk. Molly pulled her heavy wool sweater up around her ears, wishing she'd brought a hat and gloves. The cold air had a lot more bite when it swept in across the Atlantic, and Indian summer seemed to have deserted Hidden Harbor.

So had most of its inhabitants.

She had been planning a short walk from the old inn through the center of the small town and back, just enough to stretch her legs and get the stiffness out of her body. Just enough to give her time to think about Mrs. Twitchell's startling revelation.

At first she thought the old lady was imagining things. Why should anyone care about a long-dead misfit? As far as Molly knew, she was the only one who even remembered Michael O'Flannery had existed, and she'd gotten used to the notion that he was her private possession. But the unfriendly Jake had certainly taken an immediate dislike to her, and every inhabitant of Hidden Harbor seemed to have disappeared at her approach. Businesses were closed, shades were pulled.

She trudged on, keeping her head down against the sharp breeze. It had to be her imagination—after all, it was just after five. Most businesses would be closed.

And most people would be out on the streets, on their way home. Except that this was a fishing community, she reminded herself. Lobster fisherman wouldn't go by the clock.

The town of Hidden Harbor was less than three blocks long. At the end was a town green, and behind it a tall white church, its spire reaching heavenward at a slightly askew angle. She crossed the empty green to pause at the iron gate outside the churchyard. It was Presbyterian, and O'Flannery had been raised a Catholic. He wouldn't have come here during his short life. But for some reason she opened the latch and walked in.

The graveyard was surprisingly well tended.

The dead leaves had been raked, the weeds trimmed, no broken headstones or tacky plastic flowers. She passed Twitchells and Thomases, Morrisons and Matthews, Bairds and Belhams, some dating back to the seventeen hundreds. She was wandering aimlessly, she told herself, but her feet had a mind of their own. And as if she were drawn there, she found herself exactly where she knew she'd end up, in front of a stark, black marble headstone.

Michael J. O'Flannery, 1963-1983. Nothing else. The dates were right, but what in heaven's name was he doing being buried in a Presbyterian cemetery? For that matter, what was he doing being buried at all? No one had ever found his body, or indeed, any trace of him. There was nothing lying in the ground beneath the stark headstone, so why had someone gone to the expense and bother? He'd had no family left to care.

A few dead leaves had drifted in front of the stone, and on impulse she knelt and began to brush them away. He wasn't there, but she felt the strange need to touch him, touch the stone that was somehow connected to him...

"What the hell are you doing?"

She pulled her hand away fast, straightening up so quickly she almost slammed into him. It was her nemesis from the hotel, Jake the carpenter, looking down at her with all the warmth of a hungry python.

"Er..." she said with great brilliance, but he wasn't really looking for an answer.

"Why don't you leave him alone?" he demanded. "He was hounded enough in his lifetime, and he doesn't need academic groupies moping at his grave."

That stung. "How did you know who I was?"

"You look like a groupie."

"I mean, how did you know I was an academic?" she said hastily.

"Marjorie told me. You're not the first one, you know. Others have come here before you, looking for scandal, looking for lost masterpieces from the great man." His sarcastic tone was infuriating. "You're squat out of luck. There's nothing left. He's dead, go away."

"Why are you trying to get rid of me, Mr....?"

"Just call me Jake. You're going to be seeing a lot of me."

She blinked. "What do you mean by that?"

"I'm going to be dogging your footsteps, lady. We don't like people messing with our local hero, and I intend to make sure you don't cause any trouble."

She wondered for a brief moment if the man was a raving lunatic. He seemed sane enough, in a good-looking, bad-tempered sort of way. She decided to try reason. "I have no intention of causing any trouble. I'm planning on writing a book about O'Flannery, but it's about his work, not about his life."

"Then why are you here? His books are still in print—go buy them."

"I have them. Every edition. But the facts of his life inform his works, and I just want to—"

"You just want to snoop around. Weep at his grave, nose into his past, talk to his lovers."

"Lovers?" she perked up at that. "I never thought of that." Maybe it was because she wasn't sure she liked the idea of Michael O'Flannery actually having sexual relationships. "Male or female?"

"What?"

"There were rumors that he was gay, and that's why he killed himself."

The man rolled his eyes in total disgust. "He wasn't gay. And even twenty years ago people didn't tend to kill themselves over their sexual orientation. You've got an overactive imagination, Dr. Ferrell."

"So I've been told. And see, you've already proven yourself wrong. You said I wouldn't learn anything about O'Flannery from anyone, and yet you've already told me he wasn't gay. You must have known him." The more she thought about it the more she warmed to the idea. "You're probably around the same age he would have been. Did you grow up with him? Were you friends?"

He grimaced. "Get out of here. If you know what's good for you, you'll leave town. Who he was doesn't matter. His work is the only thing that counted, and you already have that."

"Thank you for your concern, but I have no intention of leaving anytime soon," she said calmly. "At least not until I find out why a few simple questions seem to throw people into a fit. You in particular."

"Don't say I didn't warn you."

"Oh, you've warned me," she said cheerfully. "Over and over again. I just wonder why."

"Maybe I don't want any more unsolved deaths in Hidden Harbor." And he turned and walked away.

She stood there, frozen, watching him leave. If she weren't so shocked she would have raced after him, demanding an explanation. Unsolved deaths? Was he suggesting that O'Flannery was murdered? Or was he talking about someone else?

And even more important, was he threatening her?

She shook her head. He was right, she had much too vivid an imagination. No one would want to hurt her for asking a few impertinent questions. No one would be forced to answer them—they could simply ignore her. They already seemed to be doing just that.

She looked down at the grave. There were no flowers and no epitaph, just the dates bringing a stark reminder of how short a life he'd had. And she wanted, needed to know why.

She started back through the deserted town, hands jammed in her pockets, deep in thought.

Lights spilled out on the sidewalk from one business that obviously hadn't heard The Pariah had come to town, and she stopped, staring into the cozy interior of Binnie's Diner.

Maybe it was all her imagination. Maybe Jake was crazy. And maybe she really needed a cup of coffee and a bowl of soup.

She pushed open the door, and voices spilled out with the warmth and the light. By the time she closed the door behind her all noise had stopped, except for the hiss and splatter of the grill.

There must have been eight or nine people in the small restaurant, most of them at the long counter, and they were all staring at her. The expression on their faces was the same—distrust and unwelcome, and for a bizarre moment, she thought they were all part of the same, identical inbred family.

When they turned away from her, she realized that the only similarity they had was their wariness toward her. A skinny woman stood behind the counter, glaring at her, her too-bright lipstick garish in the fluorescent light. "We're closed," she said.

Molly had excellent eyesight, and she could

read the name Binnie embroidered across the woman's flat breast. She glanced around at the other patrons, who were busily applying themselves to their food. Her gaze skittered over to the waitress, who looked up at Molly and smiled as she set a plate of food on one of the tables.

"We aren't closing yet, Binnie," she said in a cheery voice. "It's cold out there—we're not going to refuse a stranger a cup of coffee, are we?"

The last thing Molly wanted to do was to sit down in front of all those staring eyes and try to choke something down, but pride kept her rooted to the floor. If she let them drive her away this early, then she wouldn't accomplish a thing. And this was one thing she needed to finish.

"Suit yourself," Binnie said in a sour voice, turning back to the grill.

"There's a nice booth over in the corner," the waitress said. Her name was emblazoned across her chest, as well, though her relative curviness made it a little harder to read. It was either Laura Ann or Laura Jane, but Molly decided she couldn't spend too much time staring a strange woman's breast—she'd already made enough enemies in this town just by being here.

"Thanks," she said. She made her way through the crowded restaurant to the empty table and slunk into the seat. The people of Hidden Harbor were starting to talk again, albeit in low, hushed voices as they shot occasional glances her way. By the time Molly opened up the menu, Laura was back, with two cups of coffee and a friendly smile.

She set both cups down on the table and slid into the seat opposite her. "Welcome to Hidden Harbor, Dr. Ferrell. Don't mind the others—they're not really that unfriendly once you get to know them."

A muffled "humph" accompanied Laura Jane's cheerful statement. She lowered her voice. "It's just that everyone around here feels a little protective about Michael's memory. They're worried about what you might say."

Molly took a tentative sip of her coffee. She usually drank it black, but this stuff had the consistency of tar, and she reached for the creamer. "Aren't you going to get into trouble talking to me?"

Laura Jane grinned. "I've lived in this town all my life—they're used to me by now. All the disapproval in the world isn't going to shut me up."

"All your life? Did you know Michael O'Flannery?"

Laura Jane laughed. "Straight to the point, aren't you? Let me give you a little advice. People around here like plain speaking, but you'd still better take it slow if you want to get somewhere. We don't give up our secrets easily."

Molly wrapped her hands around the thick mug, taking her time. "There are secrets?" she asked.

"There are always secrets," Laura Jane said. "And, yes, I knew Michael. I was desperately in love with him. So was the entire female population of Hidden Harbor, young and old. Who wouldn't be? He was beautiful and tortured and wildly romantic. You're probably a little bit in love with him yourself."

Molly jerked, startled. That was the second time in less than an hour that someone had accused her of being in love with Michael O'Flannery. She wasn't, of course. At most she had a kind of silly crush on him, but she hadn't thought it was that pitifully obvious. "It's pretty much a waste of time to be in love with a dead man, wouldn't you say?" she murmured, taking a sip of her coffee and managing not to shudder.

"You wouldn't be the first," she said. "By the way, I'm Laura Jane Twitchell. Your landlady's my mother-in-law. You'll find that most people around here are related."

"Then that would explain Michael O'Flannery's headstone. I thought all his family had died."

"They did. Before he killed himself. The town thought they'd erect that monument. The people around here felt kind of bad about the way they treated him."

"What do you mean?"

Before she could answer, the door to the café opened, and Jake stepped inside. The quiet hum of conversation stopped once again, as everyone turned to look at him. And then looked at her. And then back at him, as if it were some macabre tennis match.

The moment his eyes set on Laura Jane she scrambled from the bench. "Guess my break's over," she said cheerfully. "Hi, there, Marley. What can I get you?"

"Peace and quiet," he muttered.

Laura Jane wasn't the slightest intimidated by Jake's attitude. "We're kind of crowded tonight. Why don't you sit with Dr. Ferrell?"

The audible gasp from the assembled patrons almost made Molly giggle. What the hell did they think Jake was, the Keeper of the Eternal Flame? He seemed to have appointed himself just that.

Jake simply sat at the counter, turning his back to Molly's table.

"Laura Jane, don't you think you oughta get your fat butt in gear?" Binnie demanded harshly. "We're full up and you're busy flapping your gums."

"Now, Binnie, you know you always wanted a butt like mine," Laura Jane shot back, unperturbed.

"Half of it would do," Binnie snapped.

There was uneasy laughter in the crowded restaurant. Apparently this was an old argument, one that never failed to amuse Binnie's patrons, and for the moment Molly's presence was forgotten.

She leaned back in the booth, letting her eyes wander around the room. Both Laura Jane and Binnie looked as if they were late thirties or early forties. Laura Jane said she and everyone else had been in love with Michael O'Flannery. Presumably that meant Binnie, as well. Is that what Jake had meant when he talked about lovers?

At least Laura Jane's good humor wasn't dampened by the town's disapproval. Once the others realized she meant no harm they'd come around, too. She just needed to be patient.

What was she hoping for, now that she was here? Some kind of ghostly apparition? She was much too practical for that—there was no such thing as ghosts. But she believed in spirits, memories haunting a place. O'Flannery had lived and died in this tiny little town, and it didn't take a boatload of imagination to feel his presence lingering beyond death.

She sure as hell didn't want his transparent shape to appear at her bedside tonight, wrapped in chains and moaning.

Well, maybe she wouldn't mind if his more

substantial shape appeared at her bedside. She shook her head. She had to be crazy, daydreaming about ghosts.

It wasn't as if she spent her time fantasizing about O'Flannery. Granted, there'd been a few erotic dreams over the years, but a girl couldn't be held responsible for her subconscious mind. Besides, when O'Flannery killed himself, he was twenty years old, making him too young for her. Even if he were a substantial ghost, what did she have in common with a twenty-year-old?

She glanced at Jake's back. His dark hair was too long, with a streak of premature gray. His shoulders were strong beneath the worn flannel shirt, and she could see his hands wrapped around the mug of coffee. Like the rest of him, his hands were long, lean and beautiful.

She almost knocked over her coffee in her haste to escape from her own thoughts. Who the hell did she want to sleep with—Michael O'Flannery's ghost or Jake's unfriendly presence? Hell, she didn't want to sleep with anyone at all. Sex caused nothing but trouble, and it wasn't worth the fleeting pleasure and comfort. She needed to remember that.

Laura Jane hadn't brought her a bill, so she had no choice but to approach the counter. And the only free space was beside Jake's silent figure.

He didn't move, didn't turn to look at her. She accidentally brushed up against him, and the sensation was oddly unnerving, even through her thick wool sweater. Binnie was studiously ignoring her, but Laura Jane bustled over.

"What do I owe you for the coffee?" Molly's voice came out a bit strained and she cleared her throat. It was no wonder she was tense, faced with an unfriendly crowd of townspeople. The moody man beside her had nothing to do with it.

"On the house," Laura Jane said cheerfully. "Welcome to Hidden Harbor."

"Er...thanks," Molly said, trying to ignore the hostility radiating from the man beside her. Trying to ignore the heat.

"Come again!" Laura Jane called as Molly opened the door to the cool dark night.

"Harrumph!" said Binnie.

JAKE COULD FEEL some of the tension slip away as the door closed behind her. The rest of Binnie's patrons went back to their conversations, but Laura Jane still stood in front of him, with that look on her face that he knew too well.

"Stop it," he said.

"Stop what?"

"Stop looking at me like that. I'm trying to get rid of her," he growled.

"You're doing a piss-poor job of it. Nothing like a little mysterious hatred to keep a woman's interest up. Unless that's what you really want?"

Laura Jane had been a romantic all her life, and marriage and kids hadn't changed her. "I want her out of here, before she finds out anything she shouldn't be finding out."

"Maybe." She didn't sound convinced. "You're going about it the wrong way then. You're acting like you've got something to hide. We all are. The best way to distract her is to help her. You're smart enough to know that."

"Help her find the truth about Michael O'Flannery?"

"Help her find out what she wants to know. You've got a good imagination, Jake Marley. I'm sure you'll think of something. Some cracking good yarn that she'll swallow whole and make her forget all about Michael's mysterious disappearance. You're a good storyteller."

He grimaced. "Maybe I don't feel like cozying up to her."

"And maybe you do, which is part of the problem. You forget, I've known you all your life. You like her."

"She's a pain in the butt."

"So are you. It makes you a perfect couple."

"Go to hell, L.J.," Jake said.

Laura Jane grinned. "Just don't make the mistake of sleeping with her. Not a smart idea."

"I have no intention of touching her," he snapped. "And exactly why would it be a bad idea?"

"Because sex always complicates matters. And you, my dear boy, are not the love 'em and leave 'em type, even though you wish you were. So unless you want to spend the rest of your life with Molly Ferrell, I'd keep the relationship with her platonic. Distract her with enough stories to keep her convinced and then get her out of town before she finds out stuff you don't want her to know.''

"Why don't you be the one to distract her?" Jake muttered.

"Because I don't have as strong a reason to keep the truth away from her. What's the problem, Jake? Afraid you can't resist her?"

"I can resist her just fine," he said in a cool, controlled voice. "She's not my type."

Laura Jane just laughed.

CHAPTER THREE

AFTER SEVEN DAYS in Hidden Harbor, Molly was no longer so optimistic. Jake had proven true to his word, shadowing her wherever she went, and even if someone had felt like talking to her they'd take one look at Jake and clam up.

Even Laura Jane Twitchell was proving to be maddeningly elusive, and her mother-in-law was no help, either. By the time the first week was over Molly was almost ready to give up.

No one seemed to have any idea where Michael O'Flannery had lived. No one seemed to remember anything about him, but since they seemed to know every blessed thing about a newcomer like her, Molly found she couldn't quite believe their sudden amnesia.

Jake was the worst of all. She wouldn't have minded if he'd just been grumpy. But every now and then she caught him watching her when he thought she wouldn't notice, and there was an odd, almost distracted look about him. She couldn't decide whether it was intense dislike or confusion or both.

On her side, it was even worse. She dreamed about him. Not about Michael O'Flannery with her secret fantasies of a Byronic demon lover. No, it was Jake sneaking into her dreams, her bed, when she least expected it. And when she woke up, panting, sweating, trembling, it was Jake's face she pictured.

Of course, she'd have a hell of a time picturing Michael O'Flannery. At least she knew Jake was undeniably, unfortunately gorgeous in a bad-tempered, rough-hewn sort of way. And he was around almost every waking minute. It was entirely natural that her subconscious was reacting this way. Wasn't it?

She decided to give a little more time. Maybe today would be the day that Laura Jane would get a minute away from her family and her job and finally give her some of the answers she was looking for. Maybe today Jake would finally find something better to do than haunt her like the ghost of Christmas Past.

She woke a little after six, as usual, and her

tiny room on the second floor of the inn was dark and chilly. Mrs. Twitchell would still be sound asleep, the place would be deserted until after eight and Molly needed coffee, badly. It was barely light when she got to the empty kitchen, and she was trying to decide whether she should go back and put on something warmer than her flannel nightgown when she smelled the coffee.

Her little moan of longing was instinctive, but it was enough to make the man in the shadows jump. She knew who it was before he moved into the light. Her self-appointed nemesis.

"Coffee's on the stove," he said.

She looked at it warily. "Rat poison?"

"French roast."

She moaned again, and Jake shifted uncomfortably. For the moment he wasn't scowling at her, and she realized why he bothered her. He was, in fact, absolutely gorgeous, from his dark blue eyes to his strong nose to his oddly sweet-looking mouth. Tall and lanky, with good shoulders and narrow hips, he was the epitome of what she found attractive. No wonder he bothered her. It was always unsettling to have a gorgeous man dislike you for no discernible reason.

Except that the reason was easily discerned. "Is this a truce?" she said, moving to the cupboards in search of a mug.

He moved past her, reaching over her head, too close. "They're here," he said, handing her a hand-thrown pottery mug.

She looked up at him, startled. Way too close. If he was trying to intimidate her with his sheer size then he was doing a good job of it. Except that intimidation wasn't the first thing on her mind.

She backed away from him, only slightly nervous, and his faint smile wasn't reassuring. "Stop looking at me like I'm some kind of axe murderer," he said. "I'm trying to be pleasant."

"Why?"

"Because I finally figured you aren't the type who'll give up easily, and trying to keep you away just makes you more curious. So I'm ready to cooperate. The whole town is. Ask any questions you want."

She stared at him uncertainly, the empty coffee mug dangling in her hand. ''What made you change your mind?''

He took the mug and poured her a cup of coffee from the battered pot. ''Because we're making you even more suspicious by not co-operating. Next thing I know, you'll decide Michael was murdered and start looking for suspects.''

''Was he?'' She took a sip. It was as good as it smelled, a rare feat indeed, and she moaned with pleasure.

''Stop that!'' Jake said sharply.

''You told me I could ask questions.''

''Ask any questions you want. Just stop moaning and groaning over the coffee. It's not that orgasmic.''

Molly jerked, startled. Normally the word wouldn't have bothered her in the slightest, but for some reason, in that dawn-lit kitchen it felt disturbingly erotic.

''Sorry,'' she muttered, grateful that the light was dim. ''I don't tend to think of coffee in those terms.''

He leaned against the counter, watching her. ''So tell me what you want to know about Michael O'Flannery, and I'll do my best to help you."

She took another sip. She wasn't ready to trust his sudden helpfulness, but she was willing to take any advantage she could find, no matter what his motives. "I want to know everything. I want to know what he loved and what he hated, where he slept, where he died, why he killed himself, what happened to his family..."

"Damn!" Jake said in disgust. "You don't leave the poor kid any privacy, do you? If you want to know why he killed himself why don't you read a transcript of his suicide note. I'm sure you can find it somewhere—it's public property."

"As a matter of fact, it's not," she said. "It's mine."

"What?"

"I bought the original at auction a few years ago. I have it with me."

He stared at her for a long moment. "You're a sick woman."

"It's my area of expertise!" she protested, stung. "I'm writing a book about O'Flannery—I'd buy anything that had to do with him and his life if I could afford it.''

''Sure,'' he said. Sarcasm wasn't a pretty thing. ''And you carry it with you? I bet you sleep with it at night.''

''Don't be ridiculous! I don't know where you got the idea that my interest in Michael O'Flannery is anything more than academic…''

''You're fixated on a dead man,'' Jake said, pushing away from the counter. Unfortunately she chose that moment to move, and she bumped into him.

A small sort of bump, flesh and bone against flesh and bone, an oddly seductive brush of bodies. She jumped back nervously, but not so fast that she didn't see the fleeting, contemplative expression on his face. It made her uneasy.

''That would be pretty much a waste of time, now wouldn't it?'' she said in a deceptively cool voice. ''I'm much too practical to spend my life mooning over a dead poet.''

''If you say so. You're not the first, you know. In the years after he killed himself all sorts of women showed up to weep at his grave and toss flowers into the ocean. Down at Binnie's we kept a running score. But they dwindled eventually, and we haven't seen one in a couple of years until you showed up. Why can't you let the dead rest in peace?"

"What makes you think he's resting in peace? He killed himself, remember?"

"Looking for that peace he couldn't find on earth."

"You knew him, didn't you?"

"It's a small town. Everyone knows everyone."

"You must be about his age," she said shrewdly. "How old are you?"

"Forty-five," he said without a blink. "How old are you?"

"None of your business. Almost thirty." She wasn't quite sure why she told him.

"Too young for me," he said.

"I beg your pardon?"

"And too old for O'Flannery. He was just a kid when he died. A moping testosterone bomb drunk on tragedy and the beauty of words. He would have loved his legend."

"Then why do you have a problem with me contributing to it? He's almost been forgotten over the last few years."

"Maybe it's better that way. Maybe it's about time to let him go."

"Have you ever read his stuff?" Molly demanded. "It's absolutely wonderful—it makes me weep it's so beautiful. How could you want his words forgotten?"

"Jesus!" Jake said, clearly disgusted.

"Who knows what he could have accomplished if he'd lived?"

"I'll tell you what he would have accomplished. He would have written another dozen obscure novels, each one more derivative, he would have put out a collection or two of poetry and then he would have spent the rest of his life at an Ivy League college teaching starstruck undergraduates the wonders of self-indulgent prose."

Molly stared at him in shock. "Why do you think that?"

"Because I knew him all his short life. He was a pain in the butt, too smart and too sensitive for his own good, and people like that don't last long in the real world."

Something wasn't right. What in the world did a carpenter know about O'Flannery's future? What in the world did a carpenter know about anything?

A lot, apparently.

"Look," he said in a long-suffering voice. "I'll help you find out what you need to know. I'll show you where he lived, answer your questions, whatever you want. But when you're finished I want you to leave."

"Why?"

"Because you don't belong here. O'Flannery's gone—there's nothing left for you here."

This was a strangely intimate conversation to be having with a man she didn't know. But then, after a week of his almost constant presence, she was almost beginning to feel comfortable with him. "I'll leave," she said. "When I find out what I need to know."

He didn't look satisfied, but there wasn't anything he could do about it, so he nodded. "What are we going to do today?" He leaned against the wooden counter, crossing his arms over his chest. He was wearing an old flannel shirt, faded from a thousand washings, and it looked very soft. The kind of thing Molly liked to sleep in—there was nothing better than well-aged cotton flannel. And why was she thinking about beds again? Every time the damned man was around her mind went out the window.

"Don't you have to work?"

He shrugged. "I can take the day off when I want to—one of the benefits of being self-employed. Anyway, I'm motivated to help you finish up. No need for you to linger in Hidden Harbor any longer than you have to. Winter's coming, and you've never felt how cold it can get until you've spent a winter on the ocean."

"What makes you think I haven't? And I wasn't planning to stay all winter."

"Snow comes early around here. So, unless you get a move on, you will be."

Still trying to get rid of her. His labored affability hadn't lasted long, though he was trying his damnedest, she thought. Well, two could play that game. She wasn't going to leave a moment sooner than she was ready to, but if Jake was willing to answer questions and help her, then she had every intention of taking advantage of it. She drained her coffee and smiled innocently at him.

"I'd like to see where he lived first."

"I can do that."

"Do you know the current owners? Would they let me inside?"

"There are no current owners—the place has been closed up for years."

"Do you know where I can get a key?"

He seemed to be turning something over in his head. Finally he nodded. "I've got one. I suppose I can let you inside, though you aren't going to find anything of interest. He's been dead a long time."

"You didn't like him very much, did you?"

"Back then, no. But I've made my peace with him. Most teenage boys are self-conscious pains in the butt."

"I imagine you were, too," she pointed out in her sweetest voice.

"And still am, you're no doubt thinking." He didn't seem bothered by the notion. "I'll take you out to Crab Tree Road and show you the O'Flannery place. I'll even make Binnie be halfway pleasant to you, though that's a tall order. She used to be in love with O'Flannery and she's protective of his memory."

"So's the entire town."

Jake shrugged. "Maybe they feel guilty."

"Do they have reason to?"

"No."

"Do you have a reason to?"

"Maybe." He started toward the door, effectively ending the subject. He paused, looking back at her. "When do you want to go?"

"What's wrong with now?" It was full light by now, and the coffee had only added to her restlessness.

"You might want to get dressed first," he said.

She looked down at herself with a start of surprise. She hadn't even realized she was still wearing the voluminous flannel nightgown she'd owned for more than five years, the fabric as soft as the shirt Jake was wearing. She could feel the color flood her face, but she simply squared her shoulders and met his ironic gaze. "I intended to," she said with a lack of concern that would have fooled most men.

Not Jake. "That's probably a good thing. You haven't been to New England before, have you?"

She wasn't going to like this, she thought. Suddenly she felt exposed beneath the yards of soft fabric, and for the first time she realized her bare feet were cold. "Why do you ask?" she said warily.

"Men in Maine find flannel nightgowns to be the sexual equivalent of lacy lingerie. One look at a woman in a flannel nightie can turn a normal, repressed New England male into a sex-obsessed love slave. They'll be following you around like a pack of dogs after a bitch in heat."

"You have a lovely way of putting things," she said sweetly. "At least you're immune to my siren charms."

His eyes met hers, and time seemed to stop. She caught her breath, unable to move, as she looked at him across the shadowy room. The moment stretched and grew, till she could feel the pounding of her heart, the strange knot in her stomach, and her mouth went dry.

"You'd be surprised," he said, opening the door. "I'll be back at nine." And he shut the door behind him.

She let out her breath in a whoosh. She was hot and cold at the same time. How the hell could she have stood there in nightgown, arguing with the man, and not realize how provocative she was? Well, who would have thought an old granny nightgown would be provocative?

Or maybe he was just trying to rattle her again. Make her so uncomfortable she forgot what she came for and got the hell out of here.

She wasn't going anywhere. He could try to intimidate her as much as he wanted to, but she wasn't falling for it. She wasn't going to let go of Michael O'Flannery until she was good and ready to.

No matter how tempting his old friend Jake was.

DAMN, JAKE THOUGHT as he strode down the empty streets toward Binnie's. Hell and damnation. The longer that woman stayed in town the worse trouble he was in. For some unfathomable reason she had the ability to get to him as few else could.

He could chalk it up to simple libido. He'd been in Hidden Harbor for so long that he already knew every available female. There'd been the occasional summer visitor who'd caught his eye, but he'd always done his best to keep his emotional distance, and they left before things got difficult.

It was harder with Molly, though he wasn't sure why. She got under his skin, like an itch, and he was determined not to scratch it. She was so pathetically in love with the idea of Michael O'Flannery that he should have been disgusted. She didn't even know what he looked like, and yet she was positively love-lorn. Carrying his suicide note around with her, for God's sake! What the hell was wrong with the woman? Couldn't she find someone alive and available to vent her romantic longings on?

He could make her forget Michael. It was a dangerous, deeply seductive notion. He could strip the clothes off Molly Ferrell's body and drive all thoughts of dead poets straight out of her mind as he drove his body—

Damn. He had to stop thinking this way. So what if for some inexplicable reason he found her hot? So what if her pathetic crush on Michael O'Flannery turned him on rather than disgusted him. So what?

He needed a dose of Binnie's attitude to set him straight. Women like Molly Ferrell were no good for him. No, scratch that. Molly Ferrell was no good for him.

He had strong doubts that there was anyone

like her. And anyone as dangerous to his carefully constructed life.

He'd get rid of her. Today if he had to. By fair means or foul. Because the longer she stayed, the harder it became. And sooner or later she was going to find out the truth.

That he and he alone was responsible for the end of Michael O'Flannery.

CHAPTER FOUR

BY NINE O'CLOCK the town of Hidden Harbor was in full swing. Mrs. Twitchell had already gone out on her daily shopping trip, the stores were open, the fishing boats had left the harbor hours before. And Jake stood outside the old inn, waiting for her, leaning against a large, rusty truck that had clearly seen better days.

"I'll drive," he said.

"I don't think so. I prefer my independence," Molly said. "I'll follow in my car."

He shrugged. "Suit yourself. The road's pretty rough and you don't have four-wheel drive."

He was trying to intimidate her, and she wasn't having any of it. "I'm sure I'll be fine. We have rough roads in Michigan, as well."

"Is that where you're from? You don't sound like a flatlander."

"Not originally. I grew up in Rhode Island,

right on the ocean. It's been years since I've lived by the water." She tried to ignore the faintly plaintive note that had crept into her voice.

Jake shrugged. "Guess it's not in your blood. Most of the people around here find that once they live by the ocean there's no way they can live inland. They always come back to the sea. Some sort of primeval thing, I expect. You must have missed out on the gene."

She didn't bother denying it. She only wished it were true. The longer she stayed by the ocean, the more days she spent in that old-fashioned room overlooking the water, the harder it was to face going back to the broad flat spaces of Michigan, no matter how big the lakes were.

"That what you're wearing?" he demanded.

She looked down at her clothes. She had on her oldest pair of jeans and a long sleeve T-shirt. "What's wrong with it? At least I changed out of my nightgown. Don't tell me men around here get their passions inflamed by old jeans."

"Depends who's wearing them."

"Cut the crusty Yankee bit, will you?" she

said irritably. "You can almost carry it off, but no one on earth is that rustic."

She half expected him to walk away, leaving her. Their truce was still on new and shaky ground, and she was a fool to risk alienating him. She waited for him to turn that fearsome glower on her.

His laugh was absolutely shocking in the morning air. It wasn't much of one, to be sure, just a dry chuckle of genuine amusement. "It fools the tourists," he said in a more amiable voice.

"I'm not so easy to trick."

"Now that remains to be seen. You better get a sweatshirt or a jacket or something. It's going to be cold out there near Claussen's Cove."

"I'll be fine. I don't get cold easily. I tend to have more of a problem with too much heat."

"Oh, really?" His tone was dulcet, and it was probably her own imagination that caught the sexual innuendo. And then she looked into his deliberately blank eyes and knew it wasn't her imagination after all.

The calm way he was looking down at her

made her acutely uncomfortable. "Shouldn't we get going?" she said finally.

"What's your hurry? Michael O'Flannery isn't going anywhere. The house hasn't changed since it was closed up ten years ago." But he moved anyway, walking away from her and climbing into the truck.

The man could move, she had to admit that much. It wasn't so much a feline grace, but there was something oddly powerful and yet graceful with all that carefully controlled strength churning inside him. If you could discount his gruff personality he was quite…nice.

But you couldn't discount it. At least, she couldn't, not when that attitude was so often directed at her.

"You coming?" His voice interrupted her thoughts.

The breeze had picked up, and she could feel just a trace of chill in the air. Nothing on earth, not even a raging blizzard, would make her go up to her room and get a jacket, not after he told her to. At least they were going to be indoors.

He was right about the roads, or lack thereof. The deep ruts had once been mud, now hardened into place in a series of craters and canyons that Molly couldn't even begin to straddle. With each bump and bounce she mentally took another month off the life of her exhaust system, which was already living on borrowed time. But at least she wasn't trapped in the cab of Jake's battered old truck. She didn't want to be anywhere near him. And she wasn't sure why.

Lord, she never lied to herself! Why was she starting now? She knew perfectly well why she didn't want to be cooped up with him, why she got restless and edgy and hostile whenever he turned his attention on her. She may be madly, deeply, romantically in love with the ghost of Michael O'Flannery and his lost, glorious words. But she had an undeniable case of the hots for Michael's cantankerous friend Jake.

It didn't make sense—she preferred men with a certain amount of savoir faire, of charm and sophistication. Jake was rough, sarcastic and totally devoid of charm. Well, maybe not totally. He knew just how to handle Marjorie Twitchell, and his gentle care of Davy was touching. He even radiated a certain charm with the women at Binnie's.

As far as she could see, she was the only one who wasn't deemed worthy of it. Screw him, she thought, and pushed her foot harder on the gas. She was rewarded with the worst pothole yet, and she cursed. Jake was ahead of her, his huge truck navigating the rough terrain like it was a newly paved highway. She could see his long dark hair behind the mud-splashed rear window of the cab. She'd always had a weakness for long hair, and never yet had a boyfriend who wore his any way but short.

She was almost thirty—too old for boy-friends. Too old to be having sexual fantasies about Jake. She was much better off thinking about Michael O'Flannery. At least in his case she wouldn't be in any kind of danger of going to bed with him. He could stay in her dreams, doomed and tragic and perfect.

It was taking them a hell of a long time to find Crab Tree Lane, and they drove over one horrific rut that Molly was certain she'd hit before, the bottom of her Honda scraping pain-fully on the hard surface. He was probably tak-ing her the most circuitous, roundabout route he could think of, just to ensure she couldn't find her way back here on her own. He needn't have worried—she was generally hopeless when it came to directions. She'd taken a wrong turn a total of seven times on the trip from Michigan to Maine. If she tried to get back here on her own, even if he'd gone the most direct way, she probably would have ended up at the Pacific Ocean.

The O'Flannery house was even more depressing than she'd expected. It was three-stories tall, narrow, with broken, peeling clapboards. Some of the windows were boarded over, the shutters nailed tight, though she was grateful that at least a few of them seemed intact. The day was cool and overcast, and she expected that any electricity the old wreck had ever boasted had been turned off long ago.

Jake had already parked the truck, so she pulled up beside him and turned off the engine. He was nowhere to be seen, and she approached the house warily, half expecting him to appear out of nowhere.

She stopped in front of the broad, cracked front steps and looked out at the sagging porch that stretched across the front of the house. If

Michael sat there, he would have faced town, not the glorious freedom of the ocean.

This is where he lived, she told herself. Michael O'Flannery had lived almost all of his twenty short years in this bleak, depressing house, and it was here that he'd written his final, epic poem, scribbled a suicide note and walked out into nothingness with a shotgun in his hand.

Would she feel him? Smell him? Could she touch the walls and sense his presence over those long years? Would his bed still be there? And could she lie down on it and close her eyes, just for a moment, without Jake catching her? Of did she want him to catch her?

A dark figure loomed out of the shadows on the porch, taking her by surprise. It was Davy, his face twisted into an angry glare, his big body menacing. "What are you doing here?" he shouted at her. "You aren't supposed to know about this place. We don't want you here—didn't Jake tell you that? Go away. Go back to where you came from."

She didn't move, frozen. Where the hell was Jake? Everyone kept insisting that Davy was harmless, but right at that moment Molly was far from convinced. He'd decided to hate her, there was no doubt about that, and she hadn't been able to figure out why. Unless it was the same reason most of Hidden Harbor seemed to despise her. "Hi, Davy," she said in a soft, calm voice. "Jake brought me out here. He's around someplace."

"No, he didn't," he said flatly. "He wouldn't do that. Jake says we have to protect Michael, no matter what. We can't let you ruin everything. I won't let it happen."

"What would I ruin?" she asked, confused. It hadn't taken long for Davy to decide that she was the epitome of evil. One moment she was a pretty lady, in the next, a menace to society. Unfortunately his later reaction had been the one that stayed.

"You have to stop asking questions!" He moved to the top of the stairs, glaring down at her, and she realized he was holding something behind his back. Something big. A little shiver of nervousness slid down her spine.

"Don't you think we should find Jake, Davy? He'll want to see you, don't you think? Maybe he went around the back of the house to unlock it..."

Davy shook his head, descending the first step. "He wouldn't do that. I think he brought you here on purpose, so I could take care of things for him. He can't drive you away, but I can. No one would bother with me because I'm not right. That's what people tell me. They wanted to put me in the hospital over in Sanford, but Jake wouldn't let them. He told them I wouldn't hurt a fly. And I wouldn't."

"Of course you wouldn't," Molly said soothingly. "You know, it's getting sort of chilly. I think I'll just go to my car and find a sweater." And get inside and lock the doors, she thought nervously.

"Stay where you are!" Davy descended another step, and Molly got a good look at what he was holding behind his back. It wasn't reassuring.

She could always assume the old shotgun wasn't loaded. That it didn't work. That Davy wouldn't even know how to use the thing, or if he did he was only bluffing. Her thoughts didn't help. She stood there, frozen, waiting to see whether he'd pull that gun from behind his back and aim it at her. And to see whether Jake was going to show up in time to rescue her, or whether this was what he'd always had in mind.

The sky had grown darker still, the ominous shadows only increasing her unease. Surely she couldn't be in that much danger. She didn't want to die out here in the middle of nowhere on such a dark, windswept day.

Another step, and Davy grew closer still. She could run for it, but she didn't fancy being shot in the back while she tried to escape. If she could just calm Davy down...

"Why did you want to come here for?" Davy demanded fretfully. "Why do all you people come and cause trouble?"

"I'm not..."

"Don't lie to me!" Davy's voice rose in an agitated shriek. "You think you can fool me but you can't. You just want to come and mix everything up, and I can't let you do that."

"Davy!" Jake had come up behind her, and he moved in front of her, blocking her with his tall body. "What are you doing out here?"

The menace vanished. "Hi, Jake," he said, dropping the old shotgun on the ground. "I wasn't doing anything."

Jake crossed the overgrown yard and picked

up the old gun. "Where did you get this, Davy?"

Davy shifted guiltily. "It wasn't loaded."

"That doesn't matter. You know you're not supposed to touch guns. You know you're not supposed to hurt anyone. Why would you want to hurt Molly? She's nice, remember? She's a pretty lady."

"You know," Davy said in a sullen voice.

"Get in the truck, Davy. I'll take you back into town."

"What about her?" Davy jerked his head in Molly's direction. "You don't want her snooping..."

"I brought her out here, Davy," he said in a patient voice. "It's all right."

"But we can't let her find out."

"Get in the truck," he said again. "Everything will be fine."

Without another word Davy went, skirting around Molly as if she carried the plague. Jake set the shotgun against the stairs and followed him, pausing for a moment by Molly. "Are you all right? Did he scare you?"

He sounded genuinely concerned. "I'm fine," she said. He didn't have to know that her knees were shaking. "You take him home."

"He wouldn't have hurt you, you know."

She didn't know any such thing, but she nodded. "I'm fine," she repeated. "I'll just head back to the inn and we can do this later."

The fleeting look of frustration told her all she needed to know about their roundabout route. "I think you might have trouble finding your way. I've unlocked the house—why don't you go in and have a look around while I take Davy home?"

That was the last thing she expected. "You trust me?"

"Trust doesn't enter into it. There's nothing to find." His slow smile should have annoyed her. Instead she felt that answering tug in the pit of her stomach. "Take your time, rummage through drawers and closets, snoop to your heart's content. It shouldn't take me more than an hour to get Davy settled and then I'll be back and you can pump me for all the information you want."

An unfortunate choice of words on his part, but she didn't let herself react. She stood in the yard, watching him as he drove away, then she headed for the wide front steps of the house.

The gun was still lying there. She probably ought to pick it up and carry it into the empty house, but she didn't want to touch it. It was old, even rusty, and she hated guns. From what she'd read, she guessed it was very much like the one that Michael O'Flannery had carried into the woods to end his life.

The door squeaked when she pushed it open, and the musty smell of the place spilled out over her. It was cold and damp when she stepped inside, but she closed the door behind her and took a deep breath.

Jake was right—there was nothing to find. Just a bunch of sagging furniture, worn rugs and the scent of despair lingering on the air. The house was smaller than it looked outside. There were four rooms on each floor. Kitchen, living room, dining room and parlor on the first, all with the same depressing wallpaper.

And four bedrooms on the second floor.

It was easy enough to tell which one had been Michael's, simply by process of elimination. It was the only room that still held something other than furniture. An old bookcase stood against one wall, and there were books stacked everywhere—on the shelves, on the floor, even a couple on the narrow, sagging iron bed.

She picked up the ones from the bed. The mattress was covered with a faded, ugly brown bedspread. It must have been O'Flannery's. He must have stretched out on that tiny bed and looked toward the sea, lost in dreams.

She dumped the books on the old desk, then looked back at the bed, trying to picture him stretched out on the battered surface. All she could see was Jake.

He had been right—there was nothing left to find in this sad, empty building. Nothing to do but sit and wait for Jake to return. Sit in this cold, quiet house, shivering.

She wasn't a complete masochist. She pulled the old coverlet from the bed, wrapping it around her shoulders for warmth, and she sat on the bed, looking out at the sea in the distance. She could feel Michael there, all around her, in the fabric of the coverlet, in the dead air, in the floor beneath her feet.

This had been his bed, she thought. And she

looked down at the plain horsehair mattress and froze.

It was an ordinary enough mattress, covered with plain blue ticking. And blood, the twenty-year-old stains of a life bleeding away.

Jake was coming up the front steps when she ran out of the house, the coverlet still around her shoulders. He caught her as she almost barreled into him, his hands hard and strong and somehow reassuring on her upper arms, holding her still.

"What's wrong? You look like you've seen a ghost. Did Michael's spirit decide to pop out at you?"

"Blood," was all she could say. She'd been in such a panic she was breathless. "I know where he died."

"Do you?"

"In bed. He killed himself in bed, and someone, maybe you, covered it up. There's blood all over the mattress, dried blood. But why would you…?"

"He didn't die in bed, Molly," Jake said with surprising patience.

"Then where did all that blood come from? And don't tell me it was a nosebleed or a little cut—I won't believe you. I don't know why I believe you anyway, since you have no reason to tell me the truth and every reason to want me gone."

"I do, don't I?" he said, half to himself. "I assume you're talking about the mattress in the back room? The one that used to be covered by this bedspread?" He tugged at the coverlet still clutched around her shoulders. "As a matter of fact, it wasn't a little cut, it was a big one. Michael tried to kill himself in a drunken stupor a year before he died. He slashed his wrists, but someone found him in time, took him to the hospital and patched him up, good as new for one more year."

"Who found him? Did you?"

"Not me. As a matter of fact, it was Davy. That's partly why he feels so protective about Michael's memory. Ever since he saved his life he feels responsible for it. Half the time he thinks that Michael isn't dead. He's just hiding somewhere."

"Is he?"

He stepped back from her, dropping his hands. "Don't be ridiculous."

"Well, everyone's going out of their way to

hide something, and it has to do with O'Flannery's death. Did someone kill him? Did Davy kill him? Did you?''

''You should be writing thrillers. Michael's dead and gone, but it's by his own hand and no one else's. This town doesn't need you to start rumors....''

''I'm not going to start rumors. I just want to know the truth.''

He closed his eyes in frustration, then glared at her. ''The truth is a matter of opinion. Michael is gone forever. That's all you need to know.''

She looked up at him, tense and frustrated. He was lying to her and they both knew it. ''I'm going home,'' she said abruptly.

''It's about time.''

''I mean I'm going back to the inn. I'm not leaving this town. You can't drive me away, either by threatening me or by being nice. There's nothing you can do to make me leave here before I'm good and ready to.''

''You think so?'' he said. And before she had any idea what he had in mind he pulled her into his arms and kissed her.

JAKE HAD A NUMBER of good, believable reasons for kissing Molly Ferrell. At any other day and time he could have listed them with cool detachment, and he could have convinced anyone, maybe even himself.

But not with her body pressed up against his, not with her mouth beneath his, not with the heat and need that had suddenly flared up out of nowhere.

The bedspread fell to the ground around her, and she put her hands against his chest, maybe to push him away, but it didn't matter, because she opened her mouth to his, letting him inside, and the quiet sound in the back of her throat was even more orgasmic than her reaction to coffee. He knew he was getting hard, almost immediately, and he knew he should back away from her, before things got out of control.

Why was he kissing her? To scare her into leaving, to distract her from what she was looking for, to make her think twice about going off into the middle of nowhere with a strange man?

Hell, no, he was kissing her because he wanted to. Because he couldn't stop thinking about her eyes, her mouth, her breasts, her legs, hadn't been able to since the day she arrived, unwanted, in Hidden Harbor.

This morning he'd just about hauled her onto the kitchen table and taken her then and there. That old flannel nightgown of hers was so worn, so thin, he could see the darkness of her nipples beneath the cloth. And he'd had to stand there, keeping his eyes on her face, keeping the counter between them, clutching his coffee to stop himself from jumping her. So he'd spent all that time staring at her mouth, her soft, luscious mouth, and look where it got him. In real, deep trouble.

And he didn't care. He lifted his head to look down at her, catching his breath. Her eyes were closed, and he could feel her trembling in his arms, and he didn't know whether it was cold or fear or something else. Her eyes fluttered open, and she looked up at him, confused, aroused, dazed.

There was only one thing he could do. "You want to go in and try out Michael's mattress?" he said, deliberately crude.

She pushed him away with a choked sound, and now he was the one who was cold.

CHAPTER FIVE

COMMON SENSE had nothing to do with it, only instinct. Molly shoved him away, hard, and started for her car, when what she really wanted to do was hold on to him.

Her foot got caught in the discarded bed-spread, and she went sprawling in the dirt, her ankle twisting, her knee slamming against something hard and unforgiving. Her reaction was short, sharp and profane.

"If that's supposed to impress me, you've got a long way to go," Jake said, as if he hadn't just been kissing her, as if she hadn't just felt the deep, burning need that had ignited between them. He reached down and pulled her to her feet with no more tenderness than if he were picking up a sack of potatoes.

A sack of potatoes that refused to be held. "Let go of me," Molly said sharply, and pulled away. She knew she couldn't walk, at least not immediately, so she simply sat down on the ground, on the offending bedspread, and took a deep breath.

She had a weak ankle, and it had a stupid tendency to twist beneath her on occasion. All she needed to do was ice and elevate it and she'd be fine by tomorrow, but in the meantime she was stuck in the middle of nowhere with a man she didn't trust. To top it off, whatever she'd landed on had managed to rip her favorite pair of old jeans, and her knee was scraped and bleeding beneath the torn fabric.

She swore again, finding a better word this time. Jake squatted down in front of her, looking at her bloody knee. "That looks nasty," he said.

"That's not very helpful! And it looks worse than it feels," she said, only a little white lie.

"Then why can't you walk?"

"I twisted my ankle."

He swore then, a much more impressive curse. "Obviously I'll have to get you home."

"If you could just help me to my car I can drive myself..."

"With a sprained ankle? With a stick shift? I don't think so."

"It's not sprained," she protested. "It'll be fine by tomorrow."

He simply looked at her with his dark blue eyes, and there was no way she could tell what he was thinking. Why had he kissed her? Why had he stopped?

"Suit yourself," he said finally, rising. He held out a hand to help her up, and Molly gritted her teeth, determined not to show pain.

She managed to take two steps on her own before he came up behind her, slid his arm around her waist and scooped her up in his arms. It was a dizzying sensation. "What the hell are you doing?" she demanded, breathless.

"Damned if I know," he muttered, carrying her over to the truck. He managed to open the passenger door while he still held her, and dumped her inside on the seat with an expected lack of ceremony.

She didn't bother trying to get out. She already knew she wouldn't get far until her ankle improved, and having him chase after her would be undignified. Not to mention what might happen when he caught her.

She watched as he headed back to the abandoned house, picking up the old coverlet and the abandoned gun and tossing them inside the front door before he locked it.

The truck was a full-size one with a roomy cab, but the moment he climbed in, it felt as cramped as a sports car.

He pulled away from the house. "Put your seat belt on," he said. "And don't bleed all over my truck."

"Then give me something to use as a bandage. Where the hell are we going?" she demanded as he started driving farther out on the point, toward the ocean.

"Since I don't seem to be able to get rid of you, I thought I'd dump you over a cliff. O'Flannery's parents died that way, you know. His father was drunk as always, his mother was raging, and he took a wrong turn and their car went off the road and into the ocean. I kind of thought you might like to die in the same spot."

"What?" she gasped, looking at him in horror.

He spared a glance at her, that half smile playing around his mouth. "Just kidding."

"You're a sick bastard," she said shakily.

"Takes one to know one," he responded. "I don't carry suicide notes around with me or fall in love with dead people. As a matter of fact...I'm driving you to my place to bandage you up and see whether you need stitches, and then I'll take you either to the hospital or back to the inn. Where you'll no doubt have a good night's sleep and get back to snooping in the morning instead of going home like you ought to."

"Why don't you drive me straight to town? Since you're so worried about me bleeding all over your truck?"

"Because I live half a mile away and Hidden Harbor is four miles on rough roads. You're safe with me, Molly. I wouldn't touch you with a ten-foot pole."

"So I noticed."

He glanced at her again, but she ignored him, staring out the window at the landscape beyond. They were heading out toward the ocean, and the pine trees grew tall around the narrow, rutted road, strong enough to withstand the battering of the ocean winds. There were cliffs off to the right, and on the left side the land sloped gradually down to the sea.

"I don't see any houses," she said.

"You're not supposed to see it. I like my privacy." He kept driving, and she indulged herself in looking at him.

"There's Ethan Frome resurfacing again," she said in a snotty voice.

"Hardly. Ethan Frome was willing to die for love. I'm much too pragmatic."

"To be in love, or to die for it?"

His dark blue eyes swept over her for a moment, then looked away. But he didn't answer.

"Were you telling me the truth?" she asked after a moment. Stupid question, when she doubted he'd ever told her the truth in the short time she'd known him.

The road ahead of them ended in a turn-around, and he pulled the car to a stop, shifting in his seat to look at her.

"About what?"

"About Michael's parents. I knew they died in a car accident when he was seventeen. Did they really go over the cliff?"

"They did."

"They aren't buried with their son. Why not?"

"They were good Catholics and got to be in

the cemetery by St. Mary's. Michael, on the other hand, committed a mortal sin, so he had to settle for the lesser hell of a Protestant burial.''

''But he wasn't buried. No one found his body. Did they?''

The silence in the truck grew. It wasn't even noon, and yet the day was growing ominously darker. The wind had picked up, and there was a sharp chill in the air. A chill that reached into the cab of the truck and into Molly's heart.

''No one found his body,'' Jake agreed after a moment. He glanced out the window. ''Looks like the storm's coming sooner than they thought.''

''What storm?'' Molly demanded. ''I didn't hear anything about a storm.''

''That's because you're a flatlander who doesn't pay attention to the weather. There's a nor'easter coming up the coast, but it was supposed to go out to sea. Looks like it changed direction.''

''Don't you think you better drive me into town, then? Before it hits?''

''We have plenty of time.'' He climbed out

of the truck, leaving the keys in the ignition, and headed around to the passenger side.

"You forgot your keys," she said, reaching for them. "Someone might steal your truck."

"No one ever comes out here. Even in town I leave my keys in the truck. People don't steal around here."

"Must be nice," Molly muttered. He'd opened her door and was standing there, waiting for her, hands reaching for her. Hands that would touch her, when she found his touch…disturbing.

Hell, she was overreacting. If a man kissed her it was only natural that she be wary of him. Particularly when she hadn't been kissed in longer than she wanted to remember. It seemed like years. Robert had never been much for kissing.

"I can make it on my own," she said, starting to slide off the high seat. Of course he ignored her, putting his strong hands on her waist and lifting her down.

"Do I need to carry you?"

"You need to take me back to town…." He swooped her up in his arms again. She was a good one hundred and twenty-five pounds, but he kicked the door shut and started down the narrow path beneath the twisted pines without even breaking a sweat.

She didn't know what she was expecting when his house came into view. Some kind of fisherman's shanty, or maybe a rusty mobile home. She'd forgotten he was a carpenter.

The building lay sprawled in front of them, a magical combination of angles and lines, glass and wood, mystical and pragmatic. The ocean, angry today with the approaching storm, was beyond the house, and on all sides the tall trees sheltered and half hid the building.

He wasn't waiting for her reaction, which was just as well. She didn't want to like his place, but she did. She didn't want to like him, but she did, far too much. And she was beginning to think that maybe he was right after all, and she should get herself the hell away from this town. Away from Hidden Harbor, with its ghosts and its temptations.

The house smelled like cinnamon and woodsmoke and cedar, and it was blessedly warm. She hadn't realized how cold she was until he dumped her on the sofa and stepped back.

He fit in this room, with the huge windows looking out onto the storm-tossed sea, the walls of bookcases and shabby, old furniture. The place was sloppy-male—with dishes and newspapers scattered about, and the old couch beneath her was possibly the most comfortable thing in the world.

He was watching her. Despite all the windows, the room was dark, and he switched on a light on the desk. He had an open laptop computer, and he shut the lid as he walked back to her, a casual gesture that she shouldn't have noticed.

"Take off your pants," he said.

"Yeah, sure."

"How am I supposed to clean up that mess on your knee if you don't? For that matter, you probably could do with an ace bandage on your ankle, and I don't think I can get to it with those jeans on."

"And what do your propose I wear while you're administering first aid?"

He shrugged. "I don't suppose you'd believe me if I told you you were safe from my lust-crazed advances.''

''Oh, I'd believe you. I'm not an idiot. I know the only reason you kissed me was to try to get me out of town. For all I know you might be willing to make the ultimate sacrifice just to get rid of me. What are you grinning about?''

'''The ultimate sacrifice,''' he repeated. ''Yeah, I suppose I could bring myself to do it for a noble cause. Would it drive you out of town?''

Why the hell had she even brought up the subject of his kiss? Much less where it was leading. Her knee hurt like hell, her ankle was throbbing, but all she could think about was him. ''Would what?'' she said, stalling for time.

Big mistake. He crossed the room to lean over her, and she slid back on the couch, trying to get away from him, from his closeness, which was both intimidating and strangely, sweetly tempting. ''Would sleeping with you get you out of town?''

She swallowed, trying to look fearless. ''It depends on how bad you are at it.''

He blinked. And then he laughed.

She liked his laugh. It was a deep chuckle, one that went well with the reluctant little half smile that took over when he wasn't fighting it. "You're a dangerous woman, Molly Ferrell," he said, moving back, out of reach. "I think I'm safer keeping my distance."

"In that case I'll take off my pants. Assuming you've got a quilt or something I can wrap around me while you perform triage."

"Behind you on the sofa. I'll go get the first-aid stuff."

It probably wasn't a good idea, she thought, shimmying out of her torn jeans. Then again, how aroused was he going to get at the sight of her bloody, scraped knee and swollen ankle? He wasn't going to take her home until he cleaned her up, and she really wanted to go home. Didn't she?

She wrapped the quilt around her waist, pulling it up to expose her knee. The bleeding had pretty much stopped, but even in the dim light it looked as if she'd gotten some dirt in there, and the wound was already closing up. He was right that she needed it taken care of right away. She didn't like it when he was right.

He came back into the room with an armful of ominous-looking supplies. "Lie down," he said.

"What is all this? Take off your pants, lie down. Don't you know the word *please?*" she said, irritable. Irritable because his order had sounded far too tempting.

"Would you please lie back on the sofa so I can take a look at your knee?" he said with thinly disguised patience.

"Is it going to hurt?"

"Most likely."

"You'll enjoy that," she accused him.

"Most likely. Are you going to lie down or are we going to keep talking?"

She lay back on the sofa, closing her eyes. And then opening them immediately as she felt him kneel down by her.

He wasn't looking at her, he was looking at her knee. She had good legs, when they weren't covered in blood. Nothing to be nervous about. And then she felt his hand on her calf and she jumped.

"Why are you so skittish?" he said, his

deep, irascible voice a small comfort. He couldn't be thinking the same thing she was if he sounded so grumpy.

"Sorry," she muttered. "Go ahead." She turned to stare at the bookshelves, concentrating on the titles. He had the strangest collection of stuff. Michael O'Flannery's small body of work was easy enough to find, and she wondered whether they were autographed. They must be, since Jake had known him all his short, tragic life. There were books on birds and nature, art books and shelves of mysteries, including what appeared to be the entire collection of Sydney Carton's works. She glanced back at Jake. They had more in common that she realized, and the thought bothered her. It was a shame and a sin in the academic community to read genre fiction, and Molly kept her vice secret, even when it came to a writer as wonderful as Sydney Carton. Jake was the first person she'd met who seemed to share her passionate enthusiasm.

"You like mysteries?" she asked, her voice only slightly strained. He'd put one hand under her knee, his fingers splayed on her thigh, and she was having a little trouble concentrating.

The pain was nothing compared to the feel of his hands on her leg.

"In books, not in real life," he said, following her gaze. "Not your cup of tea, of course."

"I love Sydney Carton."

He looked at her, startled. "Now that I find hard to believe."

"You must know how good he is, otherwise you wouldn't have all of his books."

Again that wry little half smile. "They're not bad for trashy paperbacks," he murmured.

"You're worse than my snotty colleagues."

"I doubt that. I'm sure you feel right at home with all those lofty academics."

"You're sure of a lot of things that you know absolutely nothing about," she said.

"You don't like teaching?"

"I love teaching. I just don't like the politics. The bureaucracy, the competition. I never get any time with the students—it's all spent on meetings and grant writing and backstabbing. Once I get tenure it'll probably be even worse."

"What did you think it would be like? High school?"

"I probably would have been a lot happier if it was."

"Then why don't you teach high school?"

"And waste my education?" she said, horrified.

"Seems to me it's more of a waste spending your life doing something you don't really like, when you could do something you cared about and help people at the same time."

His hands left her legs, and he sat back on his heels, watching her.

"Why would I be helping people?"

"Because most high school teachers are crap, but a good one changes lives."

"Maybe I don't want to change lives."

"Sure you do, Molly. You want to wade into people's lives and mess around with them and fix them, I can see it in your eyes. I'm sure you think that if you had just met Michael O'Flannery you would have saved him."

"I was eleven when he died. That's a little young for saving people," she said, trying to be caustic when that was exactly what she'd fantasized, and then she realized that he'd put his hand back on her legs, his fingers just brushing her skin with something that could almost be called a caress. "What are you doing?"

"You know what I'm doing," he said, sliding his hand up her thigh. "I'm trying to drive you away." His fingertips touched the edge of the quilt she had bunched around her. "Is it working?"

"Yes!" she said in a nervous little squeak.

"Then why aren't you running?"

"I hurt my ankle."

"Lucky me." He tugged at the quilt, and she held on tightly. "Are we going to have a tug of war? I'd win."

"You should take me back to the inn."

"I know I should. Do you want me to?"

Somehow one hand had slid up under the bunched-up quilt. He had wicked, clever hands, and before she knew what he was doing he'd slid his fingers beneath her panties, touching her.

"Yes," she said in a tiny yelp. And he touched her again, a little harder. "Please," she said.

His eyes were as hard as diamonds in the dimly lit room, and behind him she could see the storm coming down on them, the trees whipping in the wind, the crash of the waves on the rocky beach. And then she couldn't see anything at all, as his head blocked out the light and he kissed her.

CHAPTER SIX

HE'D KNOWN this was going to happen the minute he set eyes on her. He'd taken one look at her across Marjorie Twitchell's kitchen and known exactly where it would lead. It didn't matter how hard he tried to avoid her, how bad an idea this was. He'd known he was going to be kissing her, his hands between her legs, and all the denial in the world wasn't going to stop it.

The second kiss was even better than the first. Tasting her mouth again was like coming home to something strange yet familiar, a place he wanted to go again and again. Her lips were soft, tentative, but she didn't resist. She tentatively touched his tongue with hers, and there was a sudden flash of light, followed by the crashing sound of thunder, and the room was plunged into darkness.

It didn't matter. Outside the house the storm

hit with a wild, unexpected fury. Inside everything was heat.

"Don't do this," she said, sliding her arms around his neck and pulling him down to her mouth. "This is a very bad idea."

"Yes," he said, and he picked her up in his arms, dropping the quilt on the floor. He wanted to push her up against the wall and take her there, he wanted to throw himself on top of her on the sofa. But if he was fool enough to do this, he was going to do it right.

He could feel the tension running through her body as he made his way through the darkness. She was shivering, but the house was warm, and he knew she was frightened.

"You should take me home." She kissed the side of his neck.

"Yes," he said.

"Where are you taking me?"

"To bed."

She didn't bother arguing, just buried her face against his shoulder as he carried her into the darkness. He put her down on the wide bed that he'd never shared with anyone, and began to strip off her clothes, the baggy white T-shirt, the flimsy underwear, the bra that he wanted to rip off her. He didn't—she was scared enough. But not so scared that she didn't lie back on the bed, waiting for him.

They made love in silence, her only sound the small muffled cry when he pushed deep inside her. He stopped, afraid he'd hurt her, but she wrapped her legs around his hips, pulling him closer, and he felt the first shimmers of climax course through her body.

He wanted to make her come first, so he could concentrate on his own pleasure, but it didn't work out that way. It didn't take him long to figure out what she liked, the way she wanted him to move. It was easy enough to read the choking sound of her breathing, the sudden spasm in her body. But he hadn't expected her first, tentative orgasm to trigger his own, and he couldn't stop, couldn't hold back, as he felt her tighten around him with an anxious sort of wail. And then he was lost, buried in her, wrapped around her, holding her, as pure sensation swept over him, shaking him to pieces.

He caught his breath before she did. His heart was hammering against his ribs, but at least he could breathe. She was still gasping for air when he rolled over, taking her with him.

"Careful of your knee," was all he said.

"Forget my knee," she said, and leaned over to kiss him.

She was asleep in his arms when the lights came back on five hours later. It was no wonder she was exhausted—he'd done more in those five hours than he'd done in the last five years. And he wasn't finished.

She didn't wake up immediately, and he gave in to the rare indulgence of watching her while she slept. At some point she'd cried, maybe more than once. He could see the stain of tears on her cheeks. Her mouth was red, swollen from his, and there were whisker burns on her face and neck. And between her thighs.

If he'd known what was going to happen he would have shaved. He wanted to kiss her soft skin where his own had abraded it. He wanted to lick it. He wanted to bite it.

He was getting hard again, and he thought she'd probably reached her limit. He needed to think about something else, but that was a little difficult with a soft, naked woman in his arms.

Then he realized she was awake, staring up

at him with troubled eyes. She was already regretting it, ready to run. Just as well, he thought. Maybe this time she really would leave town, and he could forget about her. Maybe.

She pulled away from him, and he let her go, reluctantly. They'd kicked the covers off the bed long ago, but she fished around and found the sheet, pulling it around her as she looked at him. He didn't have much of a chance to see her body before she covered up, but he already knew he liked it. Hell, he was obsessed by it. He would have liked to have made love in the light, but clearly the time had passed.

"This was a mistake," she said.

"Yeah?" he said. "Why?"

"I don't even know you. We don't like each other. I don't do things like this."

"You just did. And it doesn't matter whether we like each other or not. It goes beyond that."

"Don't be ridiculous," she said, clutching the sheet to her. "Do you think I'm in love with you? That I have some sort of adolescent crush on you and all you had to do was touch me and I melted?''

She was beginning to piss him off. ''No, I think you have an obsession with Michael O'Flannery. You probably jumped me because you thought I was the closest thing left to him.''

''I did not jump you! You jumped me.''

''Let's say the jumping was mutual,'' he drawled, getting out of bed and reaching for his discarded jeans. ''And don't tell me you didn't enjoy it. You may have been closing your eyes, pretending I was your precious Michael, but it was me inside you. Not some dead poet.''

''Why are you so jealous of him? You really hate him, don't you?'' she said. ''What did he ever do to you?''

''Oh, no,'' he shot back. ''I'm not going to give you more ammunition for your little tell-all.''

''I told you, I'm writing about his work, not his life. What did Michael O'Flannery do to you to make you hate him so much? Because you do hate him, don't you?''

He crossed the room, so fast she couldn't

duck out of the way, and knelt on the bed, looming over her. "He ruined my life."

She stared up at him. "Did you kill him?"

"What?"

"Don't look so innocent! The whole town acts guilty as sin, you in particular. Did you kill Michael O'Flannery?"

He didn't even hesitate; he was in an ugly mood. He wasn't quite sure what he'd expected from her, but it wasn't this suspicion. "As a matter of fact, I did."

She didn't move. Then suddenly she scrambled off the bed, the sheet still wrapped around her, and took off.

For a moment he thought she'd go sprawling on the hardwood floor, but she managed to hobble into the living room at a half run. She was going to have a difficult time finding her clothes; they were strewn all over the place, and he didn't even know where she'd put her jeans. He grabbed a T-shirt and followed her, scooping up her discarded clothes along the way.

She was sitting on the sofa, staring at the bookshelf. He dumped her clothes in her lap, then turned away. "I'll take you back to the inn now," he said.

"What if I call the police?"

"Habeas corpus, Molly. No body, no death." And he turned away from her before he gave in to temptation and touched her. Because he knew damned well she'd give in, as well, and touch him back, and things were already screwed up enough.

SHE DRESSED QUICKLY, ignoring the pain in her knee and ankle, ignoring the tenderness in other, less-exposed parts of her body. She must be sicker than she thought. She'd just had the best sex of her entire life with a hostile stranger who admitted he murdered someone. She should be calling the police, and instead she was thinking of the last few hours and the feel of his skin against hers.

He was lying. He had to be. He couldn't have killed Michael O'Flannery. The people of Hidden Harbor wouldn't cover up such a crime, not unless O'Flannery himself was some kind of vicious monster—a child molester or worse—who had to be exterminated.

But O'Flannery was no such thing. He was

just a poor, lost soul with a miraculous gift for words, and he'd died too young. At Jake's hands?

It was impossible. And yet there'd been no hesitation, no doubt when he said he'd killed him. And the hideous thing was, Molly believed him.

She stood up, trying to put a bit of weight on her bad ankle. It held, just barely, and she limped across the room to the desk. To the telephone. She needed to call the police before she could change her mind. It didn't matter whether they listened to her or not, she had to tell someone, soon. Or else she'd end up protecting him, hiding the truth because she'd made the incredibly stupid mistake of falling in love with him.

She really was an idiot, she thought, sitting down at the desk. Most of her life had been spent mooning over a dead writer, and now she'd simply shifted to his killer. Next thing she knew she'd be writing love letters to inmates on death row.

How could he have done it? Why had he done it? To take a human life was something you couldn't go back from. It would haunt him, doom him, a chain around his neck like...like...

A sudden cold chill swept over her body. A chain around his neck, haunting him, like the ghost of Jacob Marley in *A Christmas Carol.* Jake Marley.

She shook her head. It was absurd, a crazy, weird coincidence. She turned to look out the windows, suddenly sick inside, when her eyes caught the wall of bookshelves. The row of paperback mysteries, brilliant, literary mysteries by one Sydney Carton. Another Dickens character.

She opened the computer in front of her, but she knew perfectly well what she'd find. Sydney Carton's latest work in progress.

"What are you doing?" He'd come back into the room, and she closed the lid of the laptop slowly.

She rose, and her ankle didn't buckle. Her anger was so strong it made her invincible. She limped across the room, straight toward him, and he didn't flinch, he just stood there watching her, an unreadable expression on his face.

She picked up his hand and turned it over. The scars were still there, barely visible, from

his suicide attempt so long ago. At least he
hadn't lied about that.

"You son of a bitch," she said softly. "You
lying, deceitful bastard."

He didn't bother denying it. "What? I was
supposed to tell you? Say, 'Welcome to Hidden Harbor' and by the way, Michael
O'Flannery isn't really dead, he just doesn't
want to be bothered by people like you.'"

"Michael J. O'Flannery. Michael Jacob. I'm
a stupid, gullible idiot," she said bitterly.

"Yes," he said. "But you're the first one
who ever figured it out."

"I'm probably the first one fool enough to
sleep with you. That must have been quite a
thrill, carrying a lie that far. What would the
police have done when I called them?"

"They would have said all the right things,
promised to investigate and keep you in-
formed, and then they would have covered it
up. As they have for the past twenty years. But
it doesn't matter, because you wouldn't have
called them."

"Why? Would you have killed me first?"

He shook his head. "No. I never killed anyone but my younger self. You wouldn't have

called them because you wouldn't have wanted to hurt me. You're in love with me."

"I've said it before and I'll say it again—you're sick."

"And you're no different."

She stood there, too close to him, glaring at him. He was everything she'd ever fantasized about, he was a wretched, lying snake.

"I want to go home."

"Back to the inn?"

She shook her head. "Oh, no. You've got what you wanted. I'm leaving Hidden Harbor as soon as I can get my car."

She waited for some reaction from him, but he merely nodded. "I'll drive you back to where you left it."

"I'm not going anywhere with you. Someone else can take me."

He sighed. "Like who? We don't have taxis in Hidden Harbor. The only way you're getting back to your car is with me."

"I'm not getting anywhere near you."

"You're already quite close," he said in a soft, seductive voice, and she stumbled back nervously.

"I'll walk."

"Your ankle won't be ready for a hike like that for days. Not that I wouldn't rather you stayed. Why don't you take off your clothes and get comfortable?"

She slapped him. She'd never hit anyone in her entire adult life, and the sound of her hand on his face was shocking.

He didn't even flinch. "Okay," he said. "I guess not. I'll go into town and ask someone to pick up your car and you. How about that?"

Her hand hurt, and she could see the mark on his face. It shook her, almost as much as the truth had.

"That's fine."

"Feel free to make yourself at home while I'm gone," he said. "And if you have any questions, just write them down and I'll answer them later."

"Just one. Why did you do it?"

"Why did I pretend to kill myself and take on a new persona? A dozen reasons. Maybe I didn't like myself very much. Maybe I was tired of expectations and pressure. And maybe I was tired of academics picking my bones. Like you. I like being Jacob Marley. And I sure as hell like Sydney Carton a lot better than O'Flannery.''

"I hate Charles Dickens.''

He sighed. "Then I guess we have a problem.'' And he walked out of the house, leaving her alone.

She waited until she heard the truck drive away. The storm was over, but the ocean still tossed in angry black waves, and the sky was thick with clouds. She stood in the window, holding her breath. She didn't know if she wanted to break something or cry.

She wanted to run away and hide. Hide from Jake, hide from herself, hide from the truth. She'd made a complete and total fool of herself, and she'd ruined her career. She wasn't going to write a damned word about Michael O'Flannery. Years and years of her life had gone for nothing, done nothing but make her fall in love with a phantom.

She couldn't find her shoes, and she was going to need them if she was going to drive back to the inn. Shoes were the least of her worries. Foremost would be figuring out what she was going to say to the university. Where would her tenure track go? And did she even give a rat's ass?

She could always tell the truth. It would be the literary, academic coup of the new century.

But she wasn't going to do that. She was going to keep his secret, and she didn't even want to think why.

The need to cry seemed to be winning the battle over self-control, and she wiped her hand across her face angrily, when she heard the unmistakable sound of her Honda. It had a high-pitched sort of whistle, the fault of tricky valves, but she knew it anywhere. Jake must have found someone to pick her up.

The hell with her shoes. She headed out into the storm-wet afternoon in her bare feet, hobbling as best she could. She wanted to be gone by the time Jake got back. Though if he had any sense he'd make himself scarce until he knew she was gone. In love with him? In his dreams!

Her car was sitting in the turnaround, motor running, but there was no one in sight. She limped across the clearing, reaching for the door, when something slammed down on the back of her head and she pitched forward into utter blackness.

CHAPTER SEVEN

SHE WAS COLD, she was wet, she was cramped and uncomfortable, and she had no earthly idea where she was. Scratch that, she knew where she was. On the floor in the tiny back seat of her car, in the dark, with her hands and ankles tied.

The car wasn't moving—a small consolation, until she realized that she wasn't alone. Someone was sitting in the front seat, breathing heavily. He'd adjusted the driver's seat so that it pushed against her trapped body.

Maybe Jake had changed his mind. Maybe he decided his secret was worth protecting, to the point of committing murder, and he'd picked up her car, come back to knock her out and dump her body where no one would ever find it.

It all made sense. Except that she didn't believe it. He might be a liar and a pig, but he wasn't a killer. And he wouldn't hurt her.

She shifted, and the car rocked beneath her. "Stay still," a voice said, and Molly had a sick feeling in the pit of her stomach. It wasn't Jake, it was Davy. Of course. Davy, who was so determined to protect his friend Michael. And his friend Jake. Did he even understand what Michael had done? Did he know what he was trying to cover up?

"Davy," she said softly. "I'm uncomfortable back here. Could you untie me and let me sit up?"

"No!" He sounded fretful and frightened. "I have to do this. I don't want to, but I have to."

"What do you have to do, Davy?"

"I have to get rid of you. Jake doesn't want strangers to know. He trusts me, and I promised I'd never tell anyone about him being Michael. But you figured it out, and I can't let that happen. I have to protect him."

"I'm going away, Davy. I was just going to get my car and I was going to leave Hidden Harbor and never come back."

"But you'd tell."

"No, I wouldn't. I can keep a secret, Davy, just as you can. I'll go back to Michigan and you'll never hear from me again."

"I can't let you do that." His voice was soft, implacable. "It won't hurt, not for long. Jake wouldn't like it if I hurt you. They say drowning's easy. You just sort of go to sleep."

The fear was like a cold stone in the pit of her stomach. "I don't want to drown."

"I know," Davy said in a mournful voice. "But there's no choice." He opened the car door, and the dome light came on, momentarily blinding her. It had gotten dark so quickly—how long had she been lying cramped in the back of her car? She could hear the roar and crash of the surf, and her panic grew.

He opened the back door and caught her by the shoulders, pulling her out onto the cold, wet ground. He was very strong, a huge, powerful man with the mind of a child, and there was no way she could reason with him. No way she could even begin to fight him.

He started dragging her through the mud, closer to the sound of the roaring ocean. She tried to dig in her heels, but he didn't seem to notice. He was panting slightly from the effort, but it was more of an inconvenience than anything else. Then he stopped, and put her into a sitting position. She was on the cliffs above Claussen's Cove, where Jake's parents had died.

"I'm going to have to untie you," Davy was saying. "And I want you to promise not to run. If they find your body with your hands and feet tied they might think it wasn't an accident."

"They might," Molly agreed gravely.

"I'll be very cross with you if you run."

She said nothing as he bent over her, unfastening the binding that he had wrapped around her ankles. He'd used an old phone cord, and the plastic had dug into her sprained ankle, making it worse. He removed it, then proceeded to recoil it in a neat little circle. Molly just watched him.

He reached for her wrists and began the same process, biting his lip as he concentrated, squatting over her in the darkness. She waited until the knot loosened, and then she kicked her foot out, hard, aiming for his groin.

His shriek told her that she'd made contact. He fell backward, howling in pain, but she was already up and running, in a crazy, crablike run with her wounded ankle slowing her down, not daring to look behind her to see whether he was following her or not. She scrambled across the rocky headland, sobbing with fear, when a bank of bright lights came over the crest of the hill, blinding her.

She slid then, going down hard, when she felt Davy's hand grab her neck. "You shouldn't have done that!" he screamed in her face. "You hurt me!"

In the distance she could hear the slamming of car doors. Lots of them. The sound of voices coming closer, the lights spearing the murky sky, illuminating the two of them as they stood perched on the edge of the cliff.

"Let her go, Davy." Jake's voice came out of the darkness, calm and soothing. "You don't want to hurt her."

"Yes, I do. She kicked me. And she's going to tell everybody about you. She knows, Jake. You can't trust her."

"Let her go," Jake said again, and even through her own terror Molly wondered whether she imagined the edge of fear in his voice. "No one's going to be mad at you, I promise. The police have promised to stay back if you'll just talk to me.''

"They'll send me back to the hospital,'' Davy said in an aggrieved voice.

Lie to him, Molly thought desperately.

But it seemed as if Jake could only lie to her. "Just for a little while, Davy. Remember, you liked it there. You had fun. And I'll visit. All of us will.''

"Okay,'' Davy said with one of his lightning-fast shifts of mood. His hand loosened on her neck for a moment, and Molly tensed her muscles, ready to spring away. His grip was still too tight, and she couldn't breathe, couldn't even say anything. "But first I have to kill her.''

"No! Davy, you promised!'' Jake said.

"Promised what?''

"You promised you would never hurt anything I cared about. Remember? You said you'd take care of the things I love.''

For a moment the only sound was the roar of the surf and the faint crackling of a police radio, and the strange roaring in her ears as she struggled to breathe. And then Davy spoke.

"You love her? Why, Jake?" He seemed astounded by the notion.

"I have no idea," Jake said, sounding so disgusted with himself that for one crazy moment she was tempted to believe him. "But I do. Now let her go, Davy, and come with me."

Another endless moment. Davy's fierce hold on her neck eased, and she fell on the ground in a limp heap, gasping for breath. And Davy wandered off into the night, heading for Jake.

CHAPTER EIGHT

SHE DIDN'T SEE Jake again. With the entire police force of Hidden Harbor fussing over her, she didn't have the wit or the nerve to ask where he'd gone. Not until they brought her to the emergency room to be checked over, not until she was released into Laura Jane Twitchell's care, did she finally ask.

"Oh, Jake went with Davy to the state hospital," Laura Jane said cheerfully. "He promised Davy he wouldn't leave him until he got settled, and Jake always keeps his promises."

"Jake," Molly echoed in a cynical voice.

"That's what we call him. That's who he is now, and happier for it. I'd hate to see anything happen to his peace of mind."

She limped over to Laura Jane's van. "So what are you going to do, try to throw me over a cliff if I don't agree?"

Laura Jane laughed. "We all know perfectly

well you wouldn't harm Jake. Davy's not quite right, you know. He doesn't see things so clearly."

"You're wrong. There's nothing I'd like better than to cause some major damage to the man," Molly said bitterly.

Laura Jane grinned. "Lover's quarrel?" she asked. "I remember what that's like. You don't like it that he lied to you, and I don't blame you. I knew the moment you walked into the diner that you two were made for each other. You need to—"

"I need to leave," Molly interrupted her.

Laura Jane looked stricken. "You can't! Your car's still in police custody. It's evidence—"

"I can rent a car. I don't know if I ever want to get in that one again. How do I rent a car?"

"I think you should wait until Jake gets back. Marjorie told me to bring you back. She's made a nice dinner for you, and you need a good night's sleep. In the morning, if you're still set on leaving we can call Doris Perkins down at the garage. They sometimes rent cars."

"I'm not waiting. I'm only going back to the inn to pack."

"It's almost nine o'clock at night! You can't leave. Not after all you've been through. It's been a hell of a day."

You don't know the half of it, Molly thought, feeling a faint blush stain her face. And that was exactly why she had to get away from here. "I can drive as far as Portland and spend the night," she said. "I'm not spending another night in Hidden Harbor. I hate it here."

"No, you don't," Laura Jane said wisely. "But I understand why you're upset. Maybe you just need some time to yourself to understand what you really do want."

"I know what I want. I want Michael O'Flannery to be dead so I can write about him and get tenure. Since that's not about to happen, I'm going to go back to work early and see if I can figure out what I'm going to do."

Laura Jane just looked at her. "You're as stubborn as my kids. There's no way I can talk you out of this, is there?"

"No way."

She sighed. "In that case, I'll call Doris tonight. She'll find a car you can take."

"I won't be bringing it back."

"Don't worry about it. She'll make arrangements."

She passed him on the road coming into town, three hours later. It was after midnight, and she was crying so hard she could barely see, but in the brightness of her headlights the truck was instantly recognizable. She didn't know whether he saw her or not as he was driving very fast, an abstracted expression on his face.

It didn't matter, she thought, wiping her face with the back of her hand. She'd be gone, and once he was sure she wasn't going to blow his cover, he'd be happy. Not that she cared whether he was happy or not, she reminded herself, swallowing a shaky gulp. And she headed west, into the flatlands, with the ocean at her back.

IT WAS THREE weeks later, Thanksgiving, the start of the Christmas season, and Molly was not in a festive spirit. She'd made some weak excuse to her family in Rhode Island—she couldn't face the holidays at the moment, couldn't face her overachieving siblings and her academic parents. Not when she was ready to make the hardest decision of her life.

She was going to the ocean. The Pacific Ocean, as far away from Maine as she could get. She was leaving her job and her tenure track, and she didn't give a damn where she ended up. She had enough money to tide her over for the time being, and maybe she'd find a job teaching, maybe she wouldn't. The main thing was to get over Jake.

Time was supposed to cure everything. It was doing a piss-poor job of curing her depression. If she still had a romantic bone in her body she'd call it a broken heart, but she decided that was giving it more importance than it deserved. It was no wonder she was having a hard time. She'd nearly been killed. She'd been tricked and lied to. And her career had imploded in front of her very eyes, and she'd had no choice but to let it.

The fact that she dreamed about Jake was merely an unfortunate side effect. A little Prozac, a little sunshine and she'd be fine, just fine.

Her apartment was already packed. She'd put most of her furniture in storage, keeping only her bed and her television for the last few days. She made herself a cup of coffee and turned on the TV. The Macy's parade was winding down, Santa Claus was about to arrive, and Molly felt the damned tears start again. She cried over the most ridiculous things. Beer commercials. Songs on the radio. Pictures of kittens. It wasn't surprising that Santa Claus would do it to her.

She switched the channel, ending up on the Weather Channel. She watched it dully. It was cold and rainy along the coast of Maine. As if she gave a damn. She wanted them to have blizzards and tornadoes and volcanoes. She wanted them to disappear in a puff of smoke.

No, not them. Him. Just Jacob Marley and the chains he forged in life.

The day went from bad to worse. She turned on *It's a Wonderful Life* and fell asleep in front of the television. When she awoke, the room was dark and *A Christmas Carol* was on. All she needed was to see the ghost of Jacob Marley rattling his chains when she would have happily wrapped them around his neck. She sat up, dazed and groggy from too much sleep, when she heard the knocking at her door.

She groaned. With her luck one of her well-meaning neighbors would be stopping by with leftover turkey, and she wasn't in the mood. She was indulging herself in misery and having a fine time doing it. Later she'd put on something mournful and have a stormy cry, but in the meantime she wanted to watch TV and say nasty things to Jacob Marley's ghost without having to explain herself to anyone.

The knock came again, and she considered staying put, then realized she had the TV turned up loud enough that she wouldn't get away with it. And whoever was out there was getting more and more irritated. She could tell by the sound of his fist on the door.

"Coming. Hold your horses!" she said irritably, struggling to her feet. She was wearing sweats, a baggy T-shirt, and her hair was in braids, and she couldn't care less who saw her that way. Until she opened the door and looked up into his dark blue eyes.

The silence was palpable, with only the muffled sound of Scrooge in the background. "You look like hell," Jake said charitably.

She slammed the door in his face.

She knew it wasn't going to end at that, but it was extremely satisfying. She waited a good two minutes, then finally opened the door again.

He looked the same. Grumpy, sexy, annoying as hell. Now that she knew just what that mouth tasted like, it was even more unsettling, but she plastered a steely expression on her face and opened the door wider. "You're bothering the neighbors."

He stepped inside, closing it behind him. She hadn't told him he could, but that seemed beside the point. "Why are you here?" she demanded.

"Mabel Barton is pregnant."

Molly blinked. "How nice. Are you the father?"

She'd forgotten his laugh. "Not likely. Mabel and Frank already have five little monsters, and I don't think Frank would take it too well if I messed around with his wife."

"And how does this concern me? Not that I'd care if you were messing around with her," she added hastily.

She thought she'd memorized everything

about him. And she had, but the reality of that little half smile hit her with the power of a sledgehammer.

"Of course you wouldn't," he said soothingly. "Mabel teaches high school English in Hidden Harbor. She's taking her maternity leave after Christmas."

"And...?"

"And we need someone to fill in for her. I thought you might be needing a job."

"And you drove twelve hundred miles to ask me this?" she said in disbelief.

"Actually I flew. I thought we could drive back together."

He looked so innocent. As if he were simply doing his civic duty. "And I would want to because...?" she prompted him.

"Because you like teaching and you're out of a job."

She didn't bother asking him how he knew that. "I can find another one closer."

"Because you want to live by the ocean again."

"I was planning on moving to California."

"California's for wimps. You're tough enough to handle Maine."

"Am I?"

"You're tough enough to handle me."

She didn't argue with that. "If I wanted to," she said.

"If you wanted to," he agreed. "So what do you think?"

"What do you think?" she countered.

He took a deep breath. "I think that I can't spend another day waiting for you to come back, and if worse comes to worse I'll follow you to California, but I really think things would work out better if you just gave up and came back with me."

"Gave up?"

"Gave up being pissed at me. Gave up being proud."

"And what are you giving up?"

"My freedom. Come back with me, Molly."

"Why?"

"You're going to make me say it, aren't you?"

"Yes."

He looked furious, frustrated and undeniably gorgeous. "All right, I admit it. For want of a better word, I'm in love with you."

"I don't know if there is a better word," she said, suddenly feeling very calm.

"So will you? Come back with me? Or am I going to have to stay here in this god-awful flat landscape?"

She smiled up at him. He hadn't touched her, deliberately, because he knew when he did she couldn't think straight. She reached up and cupped his face with her hands. "On one condition," she said.

His eyes burned down into hers. "Anything," he said.

"You change your name again. I really do hate Charles Dickens."

And she let out a shriek of laughter as he scooped her up in his arms.

Dear Reader,

I was intrigued by the prospect of writing a story for the *What Lies Beneath* anthology from the moment I heard the title. When writing a romantic suspense novel, I always try to find a topic that fascinates me and a situation that most readers can identify with on some level. The topic I chose was triggered by the question "What could possibly be more frightening than to find that the man you are married to is not at all what he seemed and that the only way you can survive is to run and pray that he never finds you?" For the story to work, I knew I'd need a brave and determined heroine and a dynamic but sensitive hero. Laura and Nathan fit the bill perfectly. In fact, I couldn't help but fall in love with Dr. Nathan Duncan myself. Hope you do, too.

I love to hear from readers. You can write me at P.O. Box 2851, Harvey, LA 70058 or e-mail me at JoannaWayne@msn.com. And you can always find out more about me by visiting the author Web site at www.eHarlequin.com.

Happy reading.

Joanna Wayne

REMEMBER ME
Joanna Wayne

A special thanks to Dr. David Cavanaugh for so willingly sharing his medical expertise, and to Wayne always.

CHAPTER ONE

Dr. Nathan Duncan stood at the foot of his patient's bedside and checked the ICP monitor, making sure the intracranial pressure hadn't climbed. Exhaustion burned at the back of his eyelids and shot stabs of pain along his shoulder blades and down his back. It had been a long, long day, but he just didn't feel easy about leaving for the night without checking in on Jack Traban one last time.

The surgery to remove the meningioma had been a slow and tedious process, and Mr. Traban's recovery would be touch and go for another twelve hours. If he survived the night with no further brain swelling or bleeding, chances were good that he'd go back to work in his machine shop, attend his kids' soccer games, make love to his wife. If not, he would just cease to exist in this world.

Life and death. Nathan faced the fragility of

the line that separated them far too often. He'd known it would be that way when he'd chosen neurosurgery for his specialty. He just hadn't known how hard some of the deaths would hit or how helpless he'd feel when there was absolutely nothing he could do but stand here the way he was doing tonight, praying that a being far more powerful than he would take over and pull the young husband and father through.

Some doctors thought they were God. Nathan had learned long ago that he wasn't even close.

"Do you ever sleep?"

He turned as the ICU nurse approached the bed. "I'm going home in a few minutes and I'll sleep like a baby."

"And you'll be back here in the morning before I get off duty."

"Doctor's hours."

"Even neurosurgeons need rest. I'll watch your patient tonight."

"Okay, but if that pressure changes or if—"

She propped her hands on her shapely hips and shook her head. "Didn't you just go through this spiel with me a couple of hours ago? If there's any change, I'll call you. Now get out of here and go home." She planted one hand between his shoulder blades and gave him a playful shove.

"Okay. I'm out of here."

He started down the hall toward the elevator. He'd barely made it past the nurse's station when the overhead pager blared out his name.

"Dr. Duncan to E.R. Dr. Nathan Duncan to E.R."

He grimaced. He wasn't on call, but someone in the E.R. must have seen him come in for late-night rounds. He took the elevator to the first floor and then headed to the west wing, adrenaline speeding his steps and camouflaging his fatigue. Hopefully, the injury would be minor, but you never knew what you might walk into in the E.R. Charity Hospital had the biggest trauma unit in New Orleans and all the major head injuries came here, no matter what the financial status of the injured.

The admitting nurse passed him in the wide hall. "Someone said you were here."

"You just caught me. What's up?"

"A gypsy in Room E."

"A what?"

"A gypsy. A costume. You know. It's Halloween."

"I'd forgotten. What kind of injuries?"

"Scratches, bruises and a contusion over her left ear. Dr. Greer checked her over when she came in. She didn't want to stay, but he insisted she be observed for a couple of hours, just to make sure she was really all right."

"And…"

"One of the nurses just reported that she'd become lethargic and started slurring her words. Dr. Greer asked me to page you, but if you want I can call Dr. Gravier. He's the on-call neurosurgeon."

"No need to disturb him. I'm already here and it's likely just a mild concussion." But it could be a lot worse. He always expected the worst. It was the nature of the job. "How old's this kid?"

"She's no kid. She's thirty-four."

"In costume?"

"Some people go all out for Halloween."

"How far out did she go to get this injury?"

"Not far. Actually she was doing a good deed. She rushed in front of a car to save a little girl who'd darted in the street. Apparently she pushed the child out of the way, but she got hit and knocked about ten feet."

"Who's here with her?"

"No one. I asked her if there was someone I could call, but she said no."

He stuck his head in Room E. The woman was sitting up, her legs dangling over the side of the bed, her white peasant blouse splattered with mud and blood and ripped at the shoulder. The full skirt flounced just above her knees, both of which were skinned. She was holding her head in her hands, and her short blond hair sifted through her fingers. A pair of bent wire-rimmed glasses lay on the bed beside her.

He picked up the chart and read her name out loud. "Jill Jacobs. I'm Dr. Duncan."

When she looked up he had the fleeting sensation that he knew her from somewhere. If he did, he couldn't place her now. "Did the other guy look this bad?" he asked, leaning over to get a better look at the swelling over her left ear.

"Guy?" She swayed a little, then clutched the side of the bed. "I want...to...go home."

"I don't blame you. Hospitals are no fun, but since you're here, I'd like to take a look at that bump on your head." He put his fingers to the wound. She jerked away. "Hurts a little, huh?"

"I'm...okay."

She obviously wasn't. "I need a better look. How about lying back on the bed for me?"

She stared at him as if she didn't understand a word he was saying. He eased her head down to the pillow just as a nurse came in. "Get me a blood pressure check," he said, trying to keep his voice calm so as not to upset the patient any more than she already was. "Then get her in a hospital gown."

The nurse fitted the cuff on Jill's arm. "Her condition's deteriorating rapidly. She was fully alert and talking clearly and coherently when she came in."

He took the light from his pocket and shined a beam into the patient's left eye. Obvious dilation. The pupil in the right eye was normal.

"Pulse is dropping," the nurse said.

He glanced at the gauge. "We're going to need a CT scan, stat. You stay with her and get her ready. I'll get the CT set up."

"A hematoma?"

"Good chance." He turned back to the patient. "You just relax. We're going to find out what's wrong and take care of it."

"I'm just...tired."

"That could be it, but I just want to make sure." He left her with the nurse. When he came back a few minutes later, the patient was lying still, her eyes closed, looking like a young waif in the oversize hospital gown. He lay a hand on her shoulder. "We're going to do a CAT scan. It won't hurt, but it will give us better information on how to treat you."

She opened her eyes and stared at him. "Nathan?" His name came out as a husky whisper.

"I'm here."

She touched her hand to his. "Help me. Please help me."

"Do we know each other, Jill?"

She didn't answer, just closed her eyes and seemed to fade into a semiconscious state. But she'd called him Nathan. He was certain he hadn't introduced himself that way.

Help me. He planned to, but he had the frightening feeling that she was talking about more than help with her injuries, and if his early diagnosis was on target, that would be difficult enough. If it was a blood clot between the skull and dura, and all indications were that it was, he'd have to get her into surgery immediately.

The fatigue lifted and his mind and body shifted into clear focus the way it always did in this kind of emergency. Later he'd try to figure out if he actually knew Jill Jacobs. Right now he had to concentrate on making sure she stayed alive to see another Halloween. To see another morning.

CHAPTER TWO

NATHAN STOOD in the recovery room, staring at his gypsy patient as she began to come out from under the anesthetic. She looked incredibly fragile, pale, her petite features making her look far younger than the thirty-four-years listed on her chart. He was so weary he could barely stand, but the surgery had gone well and that was what mattered.

She tossed restlessly in the bed, then opened her eyes. "Where am I?"

"You're in the Intensive Care Unit, Jill. The operation to remove the epidural hematoma was a success."

"The epidural hematoma?"

"A blood clot next to the skull. But everything went well."

"The little girl. Is she...all right?" Her words were slow, awkward, affected by the drugs.

"The little girl is fine. You saved her life."

Not even fully awake and she was already worrying about the child she'd saved. His respect for Jill climbed. "You're a hero, or I guess that's heroine. How do you feel?"

"Groggy." She touched her hand to the bandage on her head. "I didn't thank you, did I? For saving my life."

"My pleasure." He straightened the cord to her call button, then lingered close. "Have we met before? You seem familiar."

She stared at him, and even in the dim light, he was mesmerized by her eyes—dark, expressive, almost haunting. "I don't know you."

The feeling that he knew her was stronger than ever, but he had no idea why she'd lie about it. He stood quietly, trying to think of where he might have known her from. He usually remembered names better than faces, but he drew a blank with Jill Jacobs.

"Jill." He said her name softly. She didn't respond. Evidently she'd drifted off again. Good. She needed the rest and most of all she needed to stay calm and relaxed. He dragged a chair to the side of her bed and dropped into it, suddenly so exhausted he wasn't certain he could take another step.

The first rays of the sun were creeping into the room when he opened his eyes again. Jill Jacobs was sleeping peacefully. He checked her vital signs, then left briefly to do the same at Mr. Traban's room before driving home for a quick shower and a change of clothes. And a cup of very strong, black coffee.

Jill's face stayed on his mind as he exited the parking lot and drove toward his shotgun double in the stately Garden District. The streets were nearly deserted. Daybreak was one of the few times of day that you could find that in New Orleans.

His mind drifted back to Jill Jacobs. She lived in the Big Easy, party city. Yet she hadn't had one friend or family member present to worry about her and pray for her while she went through her surgery. She must not have been in town long, but still he was almost certain he'd met her somewhere before. He was too tired to deal with it now. It would probably come to him later.

WHEN NATHAN RETURNED to the hospital, he stopped by the doctor's lounge for another cup of coffee. He didn't have any surgeries scheduled for today, just morning rounds and a few appointments, tasks he could easily handle on no sleep. He'd done it often enough during his residency.

Dr. Carl Madison, a middle-aged pediatrician who taught classes at the med school and worked at the hospital, walked in and tossed the front section of the *Times-Picayune* on the counter where Nathan was filling his cup with chicory-laced coffee. "Looks like you made the news, buddy. Evidently someone on the scene of the accident last night had their camcorder on. They captured your gypsy woman in action."

Nathan glanced at the picture. Jill was running toward the street. An adorable dark-headed toddler in a ghost costume was a few feet in front of her, carrying a plastic pumpkin full of candy. A black compact car was bearing down on them.

"It's got your name right there in the article," Carl said. "Says you saved the life of the heroic gypsy woman."

"I was just doing my job. Ms. Jacobs was the heroine."

"Don't be so modest. It's not good for your image."

"I'm low man on the totem pole. I have no image and I barely have a life." He took the mug of brew to the table and finished reading the article. No one had interviewed him, but the staff writer had most of the facts about the surgery right. He guessed they'd talked to someone in the E.R. There was also an interview with the little girl's mother and statements from witnesses at the scene. All of them gave glowing accounts of the woman who'd risked her life to rescue two-and-a-half-year-old Jessica Gomez.

Nathan finished his coffee and decided to start his rounds with Jill. He'd take the newspaper with him. It might make her feel better to see that her actions had made the *Times-Picayune*.

"Take it easy with the gypsy woman," Carl said, as Nathan headed out of the lounge. "I've heard that if you save their life, they're yours forever."

"I'll keep that in mind."

The halls were bustling with activity by the time Nathan made it to the ICU. It was time for the shift change and the night nurses were busy turning over their duties to the day crew. He slipped into the unit and headed straight for Jill's bed.

She spotted him from across the room and smiled. Smiling was always a good sign in a post-op patient. "You're awake early," he said.

"Am I? What time is it?"

He pushed up the sleeve of his white coat and checked his watch. "Three minutes after seven." He grabbed her chart from the holder at the foot of her bed. She'd had pain medication just after he'd left that morning. It was likely wearing off a little so she should be able to talk and respond with more clarity than she had earlier.

"Game time," he said. "See if you can follow my finger." He moved an index finger from the right to the left. She tracked it without difficulty. Taking the light from his pocket, he shined it into one eye and then the other. The pupils were normal.

"How am I doing?" she asked.

He skimmed her chart. "Vital signs look good. Tracking is fine. I'd say you're on the road to recovery. Do you have any questions about your surgery."

"When can I go home?"

"Six to seven days."

"I can't stay here that long."

"Sorry. Doctor's orders. Besides you won't really feel like going home before that. Is there someone we should call and tell them you're here? Family? Friends?"

"There's no one. I'm new in town."

"Well, you'll have friends after this. You're quite a celebrity."

She narrowed her eyes and frowned. "What do you mean?"

He handed her the paper, folded so that the first thing she'd see would be her picture and the headline: Gypsy Woman Saves Tiny Ghost.

She took one look and went pale. The newspaper slipped from her shaking hands and fell to her chest. Nathan wasn't the best man at deciphering women's feelings from their reactions, but he did know fear when he saw it, and Jill Jacobs was scared as hell.

One of the ICU nurses joined them. "Ms. Jacobs has a visitor. A young man who's very anxious to see her."

Jill looked around frantically as the little color she had drained from her face. "No, please. No visitors."

Nathan had no idea what was going on, but he knew he couldn't have her getting upset like this. "It's okay, Jill. If you don't want visitors, you won't have any."

"Mr. Gomez just wants to thank you for saving his daughter's life," the nurse said. "I thought that might make you feel better."

"Mr. Gomez." Jill's body went limp and she put her hand over her chest and took a deep breath. "I'll see him."

"You don't have to," Nathan assured her. "Having visitors is your call."

"No. I'll see *him,* but no one else."

She claimed to have no friends or family around, but she definitely had an enemy, someone she was deathly afraid of. It was typical behavior for a person who'd ended up in the emergency room as a result of being battered, but Jill had been in an accident.

Nathan stood back and watched her interact

with Mr. Gomez. She smiled, but said little. The situation intrigued him, and so did the woman. He couldn't decide if it was her smile, her voice or her haunted eyes, but he was certain he knew her.

Unfortunately he couldn't stand around and analyze the situation all day. He had other patients to see. Jill would just have to stay a woman of mystery for a while longer.

JILL LAY in bed after Mr. Gomez left, wishing the foggy haze would clear from her mind. She couldn't trust herself in this condition, couldn't be certain she wouldn't say the wrong thing or do something to give away her identity.

Of all the cities in the world, how could she have chosen the one where Nathan lived and worked? Last night, she'd thought she was hallucinating, that his face and his voice were part of a crazed dream, beacons trying to lead her out of a maze.

This morning she knew that he was here in the flesh. She closed her eyes and the years dropped away. She and Nathan were back at Georgetown University, making love hurriedly so they could finish before his two other roommates returned to the small apartment.

She and Nathan had laughed a lot back then. Drank beer in that little tavern a few blocks from campus, talked into the wee hours of the morning on his lumpy sofa. They hadn't been able to keep their hands off each other. She had been so young. They both had. Young and in love.

But that was all in the past. The woman he knew didn't exist anymore. The innocence was gone, replaced by dread and fear so intense it seemed to eat away at her very soul.

She picked up the newspaper and stared at her picture again. All the precautions she'd taken to keep to herself meant nothing now that her picture was plastered on the front page of the *Times-Picayune*.

Thankfully, it was a local paper. Hampton would never see it in Los Angeles, and, even if one of his friends saw it, they would never know it was her. She'd changed her appearance as much as she could without reverting to surgery. Sometimes she barely recognized herself when she looked in a mirror.

Still, the fear persisted. If anyone could find her, it would be her husband. And Hampton Parker would never stop looking.

NATHAN BIT into the ham sandwich he'd picked up from the hospital cafeteria. It wasn't the healthiest or the tastiest of lunches, but it was convenient and filling and he settled for that most working days. Fridays were usually a slow day in the office, but this morning had proved different. He'd taken a couple of emergency appointments, neither of which had turned out to be actual emergencies, but they had taken a huge chunk out of his morning.

The doctors' lounge was crowded with other physicians who'd had the same idea he had. Grab a bite and hide away from emergencies for a few minutes. The talk flowed easily, lots of lighthearted teasing and talk of weekend plans. Serious topics broke the unwritten rule of the lunch hour. The doctor across the table from him unwrapped a tuna special, then picked up the TV controls and raised the volume. "That's your patient, isn't it, Nathan? How the hell did she make the national news?"

"I don't have a clue." But there she was, featured as a Halloween human interest item. The gypsy who saved a ghost and ended up requiring brain surgery.

The short footage had been taken by a man

who'd had his camcorder on at the scene. It showed Jill from the second she spotted the toddler yanking away from her pregnant mother and darting into the street. Jill had sprung into action but had slipped just before she reached the child. She'd managed to push the toddler out of the way but the left front fender had hit Jill and sent her careening through space. It was a miracle she hadn't been hurt a lot worse. There was also a brief interview with the very thankful Gomez family.

"She's a quick-thinking young lady," Carl Madison said. "A split second later and that child would have been run over."

"Yeah, she deserves her fifteen minutes of fame," another doctor added.

Their comments barely registered with Nathan. He was too lost in his own thoughts. If an article in the local paper upset her, a spot on national TV could be traumatic. Fortunately there was no TV in ICU.

Something about the way Jill had moved replayed in her mind. So damn familiar, and yet he couldn't place her. Jill Jacobs. He ran the name around in his mind and came up with nothing. Maybe it was the eyes that got to him. He hadn't seen big, brown expressive eyes like that since—

Since Laura Blankenship.

That was who she reminded him of, why she looked familiar. But it wasn't just that she looked familiar. When she was losing consciousness, she'd called him Nathan.

Could it possibly be Laura? The hair was wrong. The name was wrong. But the voice, the smile, the eyes, the way she moved—they could be hers.

He managed to swallow the bite of sandwich in his mouth and wash it down with a sip of hot coffee, as a rush of memories ran hot inside him. He'd been infatuated with Laura from the day they'd met, had known on the spot that he was going to fall hard for her. She'd been cute and sexy and so full of life.

Surely the fearful woman in ICU with no friends or family couldn't be his vivacious Laura. She'd broken up with him to go home and marry her high-school sweetheart. By now she'd likely have a houseful of children and a husband who loved her.

But the eyes gave her away, those and some

nebulous quality he couldn't explain. He tossed the rest of the sandwich into the trash and headed to her bedside, more nervous than he'd been in years. Unless he was mistaken, he was about to face his past head-on.

CHAPTER THREE

NATHAN STOOD OVER his sleeping patient, scrutinizing every part of her face, becoming more convinced by the second that she actually was Laura Blankenship. She looked different, but it had been fifteen years since he'd seen her. He'd been a sophomore at Georgetown. She'd been a freshman, her first time away from Longview, Texas, and awed by the university and the big city. She'd made everything exciting, thrilled him the way no woman ever had—before or since.

Her hair had been long and straight, dark as midnight then, like her eyes. Now it was blond and short, cropped so that it fell just below her ears. But it was easy to change the color and style of your hair—some of the nurses did it on a regular basis. She had a maturity about her she didn't have then, tiny lines that framed her eyes, and her cheeks were thinner, but her skin still looked baby-soft.

He started to trail a finger over her cheek, but held back just in time. That would have been a sure way to shock the nurses and start gossip. Besides, even if this was Laura, she'd come to him only as a patient, not as a friend and definitely not as a past lover. Actually, she hadn't come to him at all. Fate had delivered her into his hands, and he had a sneaking suspicion that fate was going to exact a price for this favor.

Her bent eyeglasses lay on the table beside the bed. He picked them up and held them so that he could look through them. The lenses were clear.

Peroxided hair, clear-lensed glasses, a fake name. If this was Laura, she was definitely hiding from something or someone. Judging from the fear he'd seen reflected in her eyes this morning, his bet would be that it was someone. The thought burned like acid inside him.

Strange that he'd feel so protective for a woman he hadn't seen in fifteen years, a woman who'd dumped him with no more than a Dear John letter.

She moved a little, twisted in the sheets and put a hand to the bandage that covered her head. He leaned in close. "Hello, Laura." Her eyes shot open and he saw the same shadowed fear that had been there earlier.

Her brow wrinkled. "What did you say?"

"I said hello, Laura."

"Why did you call me that?"

"It's your name, isn't it? Laura Blankenship?"

"My name is Jill Jacobs."

"If you say so." He didn't want to upset her, but calling her name had given him the information he needed. She'd reacted too strongly. The question now was why she felt she had to lie to him.

He picked up her chart. "I do need a little more information. Do you feel like talking?"

"What kind of information?"

"Just some basic facts. Are you married?"

"No, but I don't know what that has to do with my medical condition."

"It doesn't. It's for the records department."

"Why would they have surgeons gathering information?"

"I didn't want them bothering you while you were resting, so I told them I'd get the information they need." He could tell she didn't believe him. That made them even. He didn't believe her either.

"Place of employment?"

"I'm jobless at the moment."

"How long have you lived in New Orleans?"

"Years."

"That's funny. When I asked if there was anyone you wanted me to call, you said you'd just moved to town."

She was flustered now. He was doing this all wrong. He didn't want to upset her. He only wanted her to level with him. He returned the chart to its holder and pulled up a chair, determined to find a way to get through to her.

One of the younger nurses came by, smiled and walked over to join them. "Have you told our celebrity patient that she made national TV? A dozen reporters have already called wanting to know when they can interview her."

Damn. So much for timing. Laura raised herself up onto her elbows, wariness settling into every line of her face. "National television? When? Why?"

"It's not a bad thing," the nurse said. "You're a heroine."

Nathan waved the nurse away.

"What's she talking about?" Laura demanded. "Did they show my picture on TV?"

"A father on the other side of the street was videotaping his kid trick-or-treating when he saw you dart into the street. He captured the whole rescue on film. They ran a few minutes of footage on one of the cable news channels, a human interest clip for Halloween."

"Was it a clear shot of me?"

"Yes." He wished he could say no, but he wouldn't lie to her. "Very clear, especially when you were framed in the headlights of the oncoming car."

She exhaled a slow steady stream of air and hugged her arms around her chest. "It's cold in here."

"I'll get you another blanket."

He found a second blanket and spread it over her bed. She pulled it up to her chin, but he knew it wasn't the temperature that had her trembling.

"What is it that you're afraid of?"

"I'm not afraid. Look, I just need to get out of this hospital. I can't stay here a week."

"I wish you'd level with me, Laura."

"I told you my name's not Laura."

"Okay. Be anybody you want to be, but I'd like to help you. You make that almost impossible when you won't tell me what you're up against."

"I appreciate your concern. I really do, but please don't ask me any more questions." Her voice caught on a sob and she turned away from him.

He forgot protocol and standard bedside manner and took her hand in his. It was cold and trembling and a surge of awareness shot through him. Fifteen years and her touch still affected him. Laura Blankenship was hard to get over, but then he'd always known that.

"No more questions," he said, "at least not for a while. Getting upset is not good for your medical condition. I'm going to give you something to help you rest, and the only thing you're to worry about is getting better."

"I'll try."

"Good." He let go of her hand reluctantly.

He wasn't going to get any more information from her now, but there were other sources. Surgeons had friends in all kinds of places. He'd successfully removed a malignant tumor from a police officer just last year. Dutch Johnson had said he owed him a favor. It was time to collect.

NATHAN'S OFFICE NURSE, Babs, poked her head in his door. "You have a call from Dutch Johnson on line three. Do you want to take it or call him back?"

"I'll take it." Nathan slid the patient file he'd been examining to the back of his desk and picked up his pen before taking the call. "Hello, Dutch. Did you find anything for me?"

"Quite a bit. Laura Blankenship is now Laura Blankenship Parker. She's listed as a missing person, and there's a twenty-five thousand dollar reward for anyone with information that leads to her being found."

"Who put up the award?"

"Her husband, Hampton Parker."

That was not the name of the old boyfriend she'd left Nathan for. Either they'd never married or Hampton was her second husband. "How long has she been missing?"

"Eleven months and twenty-three days. Her husband was out of town on a short business trip. When he returned, she was gone. She took no money, no clothes and no jewelry, not even her wedding ring."

"Do the police suspect foul play?"

"No. According to the husband she's delusional and given to attacks of acute paranoia where she thinks someone is trying to kill her. She's even accused him of trying to hurt her before, though apparently there have been no instances of arrest or any calls to the police for domestic abuse."

"What does Mr. Parker do for a living?"

"He owns a restaurant in Los Angeles."

From Los Angeles to New Orleans. That was a long way to run and eleven months was a long time to be in a state of paranoia. But acute paranoia could explain the fear. So could an abusive husband. "Did you get the name of the doctor who treated Laura for her paranoia?"

"It wasn't mentioned in the missing person's report. Details like that seldom are. You can probably call Mr. Parker and get that information. Apparently he's eager to get his wife back if he's offering twenty-five grand for her."

"Does Mr. Parker have any kind of police record?"

"Clean as a whistle, except for a string of parking tickets and a couple of speeding violations. That's about it, Dr. Duncan."

"I appreciate you checking into this for me, Dutch."

"Do you know Mrs. Parker?"

"I used to, a long time ago."

"So, why the interest now? Have you seen her?"

"Not since we were in college together. I ran into a mutual friend the other day and he said he'd heard she was in some kind of trouble. He couldn't remember exactly what, but I guess it was that she was missing."

The lie came so easy it surprised him, but there was no way he was turning Laura over to the husband she'd run away from, not until he found out a lot more about the situation. He'd give her a day or two to recover, then he'd demand a few answers.

For now, he just wanted to see her again, assure himself she was okay. But he'd have to be careful. He'd already felt a stirring of passion, a glimpse of the hunger for her that had consumed him when he was nineteen. He wanted no part of that now. She was another man's wife and he'd already suffered more than enough heartbreak at her hands.

NATHAN STARED at the empty hospital bed and felt the panic swell inside him. The gray blanket was thrown back and the railing was down. He wasted no time in finding the nurse in charge. "Where's Jill Jacobs?"

"She's still in bed 6E, just like she's been all day."

"She's not there."

"She has to be. I checked on her just a minute ago."

"She's not there now." He rushed into the hall without wasting time arguing. He should have known she'd pull something like this. She was on the run, and thanks to the story that had aired on television today, millions of people knew exactly where to find her, that is if they figured out that Jill Jacobs was actually Laura Blankenship.

She's just a patient. The past is over and done with, and she didn't want me then, so there's no reason to think she wants my help now. The words echoed in his mind, but his body didn't believe them. His pulse was racing and he had a sinking sensation in the pit of his stomach. This was probably the way her husband felt all the time, searching the country for her, not knowing where she was or if she was still alive.

And she might not be alive long if he didn't find her soon. She'd had major surgery less than twenty-four hours ago and she was in no condition to take off on her own.

He rounded the corner in the hall and started down another corridor. He started to run. If she'd made it to the elevator, she could be anywhere, or else she could be passed out in some dark corner of the hospital needing medical care, too weak to call for help.

He was almost to the elevator himself when he spotted Laura, crumpled in a heap on the floor, the blue hospital gown sliding off her shoulders. He raced to her, knelt down and checked her pulse.

"Help me, Nathan. I have to get out of here. Please, help me."

Her cries tore into him like shards of jagged glass. He picked her up and cradled her in his arms as he would a small child. "I'm trying to help you, Laura. But you have to work with me."

The trip down the hall had sapped all her strength and left her too weak to fight him. She rested her head on his shoulder and he felt the silky softness of her hair as it brushed against his chin.

A ragged ache settled inside him. The years, the heartache, the distances that had separated them faded into nothingness. He was holding Laura in his arms and he'd die before he let anyone hurt her.

He carried her back to her bed and gently lay her on top of the covers while he reattached her to the monitors. A nurse came over and offered to help, but he wanted to do it all himself. He had to keep his hands busy while he decided how to tell Laura what he'd found out from Dutch. When he had her resettled, he took her hand in his. Part doctor, part past lover, part friend. It made for an awkward situation.

He leaned in close and kept his voice low. "We need to talk, Laura, and don't start with the Jill routine. I know it's you and that you've run away from your husband. I know all about Hampton Parker, too."

"How could you?"

"All it took was a phone call to the right person. But don't worry. It can stay our secret."

"Thanks."

So she wasn't going to argue. That would make things easier.

"How did you know it was me?" she asked.

"I didn't at first. I only knew that you seemed familiar. I didn't figure it out until I saw you on TV."

She grimaced. "And if you did, then other people will, too."

"Not necessarily. The film only ran a few seconds. I had the advantage of having just been with you all night in the operating room."

"It's been a long time," she said.

"Fifteen years."

"You look good."

"So do you. Different, but still good."

"I always knew you'd make a wonderful doctor. I used to tell you that, remember?"

"I remember." He remembered everything. How could he not? He'd relived every moment they'd spent together for months after she'd left him, had tried to learn to hate her for all the pain she'd caused him, but he'd never been able to. "Where were you trying to go when I found you in the hall?"

"Anywhere but here."

"You're probably safer here than anywhere else."

"I might have been before half the country found out I was here."

"Is it your husband you're afraid of?"

"Don't ask these questions, Nathan. You don't want to know the answers."

"I want to help."

"You saved my life and that's enough. I don't want to drag you into my problems."

"I'm already there, Laura. I can't just turn my back on you when it's obvious you're scared to death of this man."

"You *can* turn your back and you must. I'm Jill Jacobs and you're my surgeon. You can leave it at that."

Only he couldn't, not now. He wasn't sure what his motive was, but he knew he couldn't just leave her to deal with this alone. "You need to get some rest, Laura. We'll talk later."

"Nothing will change, Nathan."

He put his hand to her forehead. "Just get some rest, and promise me you'll stay in this bed. If you don't, I'll have you tied down."

"I promise."

He didn't believe her, but he was going to make certain she didn't run again. He'd hire a full-time nurse to look after her and hold her down if need be. He gave Laura something to help her rest, then stayed with her until she fell asleep. The patient-doctor relationship was strained to the breaking point. He'd never been able to think objectively where she was concerned, and he certainly couldn't now.

Still, he'd hold on to some semblance of protocol and some pretense of control. She wasn't his to love, but he was the only person she had on her side, and he wouldn't fail her.

But heaven help him if he fell in love with her all over again.

THE WEEKEND WENT as well as Nathan could have hoped for. Laura kept her promise not to try to run again and her condition continued to improve. By Sunday night, she was ready to move from ICU to a private room. Nathan handpicked burly male nurses to stay with her around the clock, telling them she was to have absolutely no visitors unless he okayed them. So far they had turned away at least a half dozen reporters but no one else.

Laura had begun to relax a little and he'd started to see traces of the enthusiastic, easy-going woman she'd been in college. She still clammed up the minute he mentioned her husband, but Nathan hadn't given up on trying to get her version of what had made her run away from Hampton Parker rather than just ask for a divorce.

He tried not to analyze his feelings for her too closely, afraid that if he did, he'd be alarmed at what he discovered. It was enough that she was here and that they were talking and learning about each other all over again. At least it was enough for now.

He saved her room until last on his morning

rounds. That way he could dismiss the interns who made rounds with him and spend time alone with her. Nathan picked up his pace as he neared her room and finger combed his hair as he walked through her door. She was sitting up in bed, her breakfast tray in front of her. A smile touched her lips and lit up her gorgeous eyes when he entered.

"Good morning, Dr. Duncan."

"You're in a good mood this morning."

"I like my new room. I have my own window."

He went over and looked out. "And a marvelous view of the parking lot and beyond that Interstate 10."

"I still like it, and I see a tree."

It was little more than a shrub, but if it made Laura happy, he was glad. "I'll be here for a few minutes," he said, directing his words to the nurse who was standing near the back wall. "Feel free to take a break."

"Thanks. I'll go grab a cup of coffee. What time do you want me back here?"

"Twenty minutes or so. I need to talk to Ms. Jacobs about the type of care she'll need once she leaves the hospital."

"Twenty minutes it is."

He was certain the nurse knew that he wanted to be alone with his patient and that it was more than her health he was interested in. The floor nurses had surely noticed, as well, that he spent an exorbitant amount of time with her. Gossip was probably flying about him and the gypsy woman. It would just have to fly. He was single and as far as they knew, she was, too. And liking a beautiful woman wasn't a crime, not even for surgeons.

He checked her chart. It had been over twelve hours since she'd had anything for pain. "Did you sleep well last night?"

"Yes. It was the first night in as long as I can remember that I had no bad dreams."

"That helps explain your bright smile." However it didn't add up with the story Hampton had told the police. If she was delusional and suffering from paranoia, she must have been on medication to help control the condition. She wasn't taking the medication now, so her mental and emotional condition should be deteriorating, not improving.

"Were you on any medications before your accident?"

"An occasional aspirin."

"That was it?"

"Unless my sinuses were giving me fits."

"Have you ever taken any type of tranquilizers or antidepressants?"

"No, though Hampton had his physician prescribe something for what he referred to as my anxiety attacks. I flushed them down the toilet while he was at work and replaced them with vitamin C."

"Were you anxious?"

"Pretty much all the time in the months before I left. I never knew what mood Hampton would be in when he came home from the restaurant. It was like walking though land mines. One bad step and hell might break loose. Unless there were people around. When we had guests, he was always a perfect gentleman." She pushed her breakfast tray aside, though she'd barely touched the food. "Let's not spoil the morning talking about Hampton. I don't know why I brought him up."

"Sometimes talking helps."

"Only if it can change things."

But he wasn't quite ready to let the topic die. "Did Hampton physically hurt you?"

"Not in the beginning."

"But he did later?"

"Sometimes."

"Did you ask him for a divorce?"

"Men like Hampton don't get a divorce. If something belongs to them, it just does. People, money, possessions. It's all the same. Now, let's drop the subject. I don't want to think or talk about him anymore."

"You can trust me, Laura. I hope you know that."

"I do trust you. I just don't see how it helps to bring up the problems I escaped from."

"Because you haven't escaped. You live in constant fear of this man."

Her muscles tensed, and her mouth drew into tight lines. "I don't want you involved in this, Nathan. You think because you're smart and good that you can handle Hampton, but those are the very reasons why you can't. He doesn't play by those rules. He doesn't play by any rules."

But Nathan was already involved. "The only way you can put this behind you is if you deal with him. You can't spend your life running away."

"You don't know Hampton and you don't

know the situation, Nathan, so don't tell me what I have to do. I appreciate your offer of help, but I have to do this on my own.''

He nodded, but that didn't mean he understood. She was scared to death and yet she didn't want his help. But he couldn't just walk away from this. She'd be leaving the hospital in a few days and he knew she'd disappear again, and he'd never be able to find her. He didn't even know if she had money to live on.

''It must be difficult to get a job with a fake name and no social security number.''

''I can usually find something requiring menial labor. I don't mind. Hard work makes me tired enough to sleep at night.''

''Do you have money?''

''I had thirty thousand dollars when I ran. It was left over from my mother's life insurance. I was saving it in case one of my brothers or sisters needed it, but I've used about half of it in the past year. Hampton didn't know I had it. If he had, he would have insisted I sign it over to him. Control was a big issue between us. I had none.''

He paced the room, then went to stand by her bed. ''I can give you money. If you won't let me do anything else, at least let me do that for you."

She reached out and linked her hand with his. "You've done more than you'll ever know, Nathan, just by being you. I'd begun to think the whole world had gone mad and I was crazy to keep trying to hang on. But it's not the world that's crazy. If it were, there wouldn't be people like you."

He bent and touched his lips to her forehead. It was a distant second for what he wanted to do, what he ached to do. He wanted to kiss her full on the lips and tell her that his world had never been the same since the day she'd walked out of it. But he couldn't let his need for her override his judgment or his responsibility as her doctor. Most of all, he didn't want to frighten her out of his life.

They talked until the nurse returned, not about her husband or fear or anything else unpleasant, but about friends they'd had at Georgetown and how Nathan had wound up in New Orleans, teaching at the med school and working on the staff at Charity Hospital.

"Anything I can get you?" he asked when

he had to leave or else be late for his first appointment.

"Yes. A big, greasy cheeseburger with an order of fries. *Not* from the hospital cafeteria."

"For breakfast?"

"Lunch would do."

"I can handle that. One cheeseburger in paradise coming up."

"It would be quite a stretch to call this place paradise," the nurse said, sporting a big smile.

Maybe it would for him, but as long as Laura was here, it was damn near paradise for Nathan. Which meant it would be hell when she left, but he wasn't going to deal with that just yet.

HAMPTON PARKER stood on the porch of his palatial home overlooking the Pacific Ocean and stared at the water as it pounded the rocky shore. A lot of women would give everything they owned to live like this. Laura had run off and left it, disappearing like a cockroach surprised by the light.

She was probably scratching around in some grimy, cheap apartment tonight, wondering where her next meal was coming from. He

should be glad she was gone, glad he didn't
have to put up with her pretending to love him
when all the time she was plotting and schem-
ing to desert him.

The thought was like a cancerous growth
that ate away at him day and night, slowly
driving him mad. It even affected his business.
After opening five restaurants and turning them
into huge moneymaking ventures, the newest
one was eating up the profits the others had
made for him.

It was Laura's fault. She knew how much
he loved her, knew he'd go out of his mind
without her, and still she'd disappeared without
even saying goodbye.

She was probably with someone else tonight. Flaunting herself in front of him, making
him want her the way she'd made Hampton
want her. Pretending to be all fresh and innocent when she had the heart of a prostitute.

But she wouldn't make a fool of him for
much longer. Sam Bailey was the best private
investigator in the business and Hampton was
paying him top dollar to find Laura. When he
did, she'd better not be with another man.

Anger boiled inside him, knotted his muscles and stretched his nerves into thin, harried wires. If he found her with someone else, he'd kill them both. He should have done that before. He'd let Laura live that time, but he wouldn't make that same mistake again.

The moon shrank behind a cloud and the night turned pitch-black. He walked to the edge of the water and felt the spray on his face, cold and prickly the way it had been the night he'd dumped Tim's body into the churning, seething ocean.

"One day soon, Laura. I'll find you one day soon. And when I do, you'll pay for all you've put me through when all I ever did wrong was love you too much."

One day soon. That thought was the only thing that kept him sane.

THE NIGHT WAS DARK, moonless, touched by an eerie stillness that seemed almost alive as Laura walked the dark New Orleans street. She'd been walking for hours, all through the night, searching for her apartment, but the streets and houses all looked the same and none of them were hers.

Her legs ached and her head had begun to

throb. She wasn't supposed to walk this far, but she had to get home, had to get her things and start running again. Hampton knew where she was and he was coming for her.

Footsteps sounded behind her and someone called her name. It was Hampton. She tried to scream, but the sound clogged in her throat and wouldn't come out. All she could do was run. She took off without looking back.

Her feet pounded against the rough pavement, slipping on loose rocks and crushing the dead leaves that had fallen from the giant oaks. Her heart hammered in her chest, beating so fast and hard she thought it might break through her chest.

She was running as fast as she could, but the footsteps were getting closer. There was no way to escape. Her husband was going to kill her the way she always knew he would. Unable to breathe, she fell against a tree trunk and crumpled to the bed of roots and hard earth, waiting for his hands to wrap around her neck.

She waited, but there was no kiss of death, no rough touch on her flesh.

Gradually, she pulled out of the nightmare. She wasn't on the street. She was still in the hospital and if she opened her eyes, she'd find that everything was okay. Except her heart wouldn't slow down and her breath still came in excruciating gasps.

But it was only a bad dream. She had to get control of her mind and her body. Slowly she opened her eyes and then she screamed. She'd been wrong. The nightmare was real.

CHAPTER FOUR

"LAURA, IT'S OKAY. It's only me."

"Nathan?"

Her voice was weak and quivering, and it was all he could do not to take her in his arms and console her. "I didn't mean to frighten you."

She lay quietly for a few moments before she spoke again. "What are you doing here?"

"I couldn't sleep so I drove back to the hospital."

"What time is it?"

"A few minutes after four." He pulled up a chair. "Are you all right? You were thrashing in your sleep, and I was afraid you were in pain. A few minutes more of that and I was going to wake you."

"I was having a bad dream."

"Starring Hampton?"

"As always. But it's the first one I've had

in several nights. I was hoping I was getting past them.''

"Maybe you're worried about leaving the hospital tomorrow.''

"A little, though I know it's time.''

She took his hand and he felt his chest tighten. He could never feel her touch without experiencing the surge of all the old desires.

"I'll miss you, Nathan.''

"We don't have to stop seeing each other just because the hospital discharges you.''

"I have nothing to offer you but a lot of baggage that you didn't pack and you don't deserve.''

"I don't mind.''

"You would in time.''

"Will you stay in New Orleans?''

"No.''

"Where will you go?''

"A new town. Someplace where no one knows me and can't connect me to the gypsy woman who had her moment of glory on the national news.''

"Then you still think Hampton may be able to find you from that film footage?''

"It's possible, and I'm not willing to take chances."

"It must have been hell for you living with him, and yet you stayed three years. Why did you?"

"I thought we agreed not to talk about Hampton."

"I'm just struggling to understand all of this. I remember how independent you were at eighteen and I can't imagine you letting yourself become involved with someone who'd fill you with such fear."

"He wasn't like that in the beginning."

"What was he like when you fell in love with him?"

She stared into space as if she were trying to remember. "He was charming, rich, sophisticated and he treated me like a princess. I knew he was jealous, but then it seemed romantic and exciting to have someone like that so enthralled by me that he hated to have another man make passes at me."

"How long did it take before the real Hampton appeared?"

"The first episode was four months after the wedding. His restaurant was included in the top ten best places to eat in Texas. He came home in the middle of the day to give me the news and found me talking to the bachelor who lived next door. I tried to explain that the guy had come over to help me get a lizard out of the house, but Hampton didn't buy it.''

"You were always scared to death of anything that crawled."

"Not anymore. Even spiders don't seem dangerous now. It's all in the perspective."

"What happened when Hampton arrived and found a man on the scene?"

"He was nice as could be until the guy left, then he went berserk. I'll never forget that first time. The veins in his forehead popped out like blue cords and his eyes were wild and beastly. I tried to reason with him, but he knocked me aside and picked up my favorite crystal vase and slung it against the hearth."

Laura trembled and seemed to curl into a ball, as if she were trying to crawl back inside herself and get away from the memories.

"Did he hit you?"

She shook her head. "No. He destroyed something I treasured. The next day he brought me flowers and told me he was sorry. That became the pattern. Erupt in fury, destroy and then apologize. At first the eruptions only occurred every few months. During the last year, they became much more frequent and they always came without warning. I'd think everything was fine and some little incident would set him off.''

"And still you stayed with him?''

"He was my husband, Nathan. I'd said vows to stay with him through sickness and health, and I believed he was sick. I begged him to go for counseling so that he could get help in controlling his anger.''

"Did he?''

"A time or two, but he always found a reason to quit after a few sessions.''

"You stayed with him for three years and then you ran. Something big must have triggered that move.''

"His best friend stopped by the house one day while Hampton was at work, half-loaded and reeking of bourbon. Tim had broken up with the woman he'd been living with a few days earlier and he was having a really hard go if it. I didn't let him inside, but I couldn't turn him away, either, not when he was hurting so badly. Hampton and I were living on the ocean south of Los Angeles so I suggested to Tim that we take a walk along the shore. When we got back to the house, he made a drunken move on me. He would have never done it sober.''

"Did you tell Hampton what happened?''

"No way! But he came home unexpectedly and found us at the precise moment when Tim was trying to kiss me. He flew into a rage, started screaming obscenities and tried to choke Tim. Tim got away from him and Hampton came after me. I thought for sure he'd kill me, but somehow I managed to get away from him and to the car. I drove to a friend's house in town, and didn't come home until the next evening. That's when I discovered that he'd...that he'd...''

Laura shuddered, seemed unable to finish her sentence. Nathan couldn't stand it any longer. He sat on the side of the bed and took her in his arms. "It's okay, Laura. You don't have to tell me the rest. It's over. You don't have to deal with Hampton ever again, at least not on his terms.''

"I wish I was sure of that.''

"Do you still love him?"

"Love? No. That died early on in the marriage, if it ever existed. What love I had was for the man who courted me. The man I married was a frightening stranger. But after that night I couldn't bear to look at him." She snugged closer into Nathan's arms as if needing his support. "Hampton killed my German shepherd. Leopold was a dog. He'd never hurt anyone, but Hampton knew how much I loved Leopold, and he killed him." The last of her words got caught up in a sob.

"Oh, Laura." He didn't know what to say so he just held her while she cried. He understood the fear now and knew it was sadness that haunted her eyes.

"I'm glad you ran and glad you ended up here. I'm just sorry it took an accident for you to find me."

"I didn't run at first. I asked for a divorce. Hampton exploded, told me that if I ever mentioned divorce again he'd kill me just the way he'd killed my Leopold. He said I belonged to him and that he'd see me dead before he'd let another man have me. He meant it, Nathan.

I've never doubted for a minute that he'll do just as he threatened.''

"I understand why you're afraid of him, Laura. He's dangerously ill or else he's totally evil, but you can't keep running all your life.''

"If I don't keep running, I won't have a life.''

"We can fight him together. Stay with me, Laura. Let me help you work though this.''

"I can't. Don't you see? If I stay with you, he'll come after you the way he went after Tim and after Leopold. He'll kill you, too, Nathan. He will, and nothing you or I can do will stop him.''

He did see. He saw a lot of things now. Laura hadn't wanted him to get involved with her because she was afraid for him. Only he wasn't nearly as afraid of a madman as he was of losing Laura again.

"Go home with me tomorrow, Laura.''

"You know I can't do that.''

"You don't have to stay forever, and I won't expect anything of you except that you let me take care of you while you finish healing. You're in no condition to keep running right now.''

"I'm nothing but trouble, Nathan. Why do you want me there?"

Because he'd always wanted her there. Because the feelings from fifteen years ago were so real he could taste them. "For old times' sake."

"I hope you won't be sorry."

"Is that a yes?"

"Who could say no to the man who saved her life?"

He heard footsteps at the door. "Sounds like Nurse Gilbert has returned."

"What do you think he'd say if he found me in your arms?"

"Nothing. But he'd think I was one hell of a lucky man." He ached to touch his lips to hers, but one kiss would never be enough. Besides when he kissed her, he wanted to know that it was what she wanted. She'd been through too much to have him take advantage of the situation just because his own hormones fired like rockets every time he looked at her.

"Go back to sleep," he whispered as Gilbert stepped back into the room. "And no more nightmares. Doctor's orders."

"Yes, sir."

He spoke to Gilbert briefly, then took the elevator to the parking garage. He had a million things to do. He needed flowers for the guest room and food in the pantry and the refrigerator. Laura Blankenship was back in his life and she would be staying in his house.

It didn't mean anything monumental. They hadn't even kissed and she probably had no idea that he was falling in love with her all over again, if in fact he'd ever fallen out of love with her. But she would be with him and he could take care of her and keep her safe.

He doubted Hampton Parker was still looking for her, but if he was, he was more than welcome to show his face. Nathan would be only too happy to punch it in for him, though a right hook wasn't nearly enough payback for the pain he'd caused Laura. Actually, killing Hampton would be too good for the man, but Nathan's job was saving lives. He'd leave vengeance to someone else.

"HAPPY going-home-from-the-hospital day. I brought you a present." Nathan tried to hand her the beautifully wrapped package he held in his hands.

A chilling wave of uneasiness crept inside her, and she stepped away.

Nathan tossed the package to the bed. "Did I do something wrong? I always thought presents were a good thing."

"They used to be. I've just grown a little gun-shy over the last three years. A present from Hampton usually meant something else to be destroyed the first time he became upset with me."

"Hampton's a thing of the past."

He made the statement with authority, but then he didn't know Hampton. "Would you open it for me?"

"Sure."

He tore the paper from the box and lifted the lid. Pushing aside her groundless fears, she walked over, lifted the tissue and peeked at her surprise.

"A dress." She held it up. It was denim with buttons down the front and a full skirt. Cuter than anything she'd owned since she'd left Hampton.

"Do you like it?"

"I love it. And it's the right size."

"That was a lucky guess. I found a salesclerk about your size and she told me she wore a six so I went with a six.''

She held the dress to her shoulders and made a few turns as if she were on a catwalk.

Nathan gave a low wolf whistle. "I must say it looks better than your hospital gown."

"So would a flour sack."

"I looked for a flour sack. They were all out. Why don't you slip into the dress? I have a couple of patients to see and then I'll take an early lunch break and drive you to my place."

"There's still time to change your mind."

"Not a chance. I'll be back by eleven-thirty."

He was smiling as he left, not bothering to hide his enthusiasm. Guilt swept through her. Nathan had everything going his way and she had no business letting him rescue her when it could mean he'd become a target for Hampton's jealousy. She'd go with him, but she'd stay just long enough to get her strength back so that she could move on.

Nathan would probably be ready for her to leave. He was enchanted by a memory, still saw her the way she'd been at Georgetown, innocent and optimistic, with dreams to match his own. Love could live forever in memories because the people never changed. Life didn't harden them and make them suspicious and so afraid that they couldn't even accept a present graciously.

She had her own memories and she'd keep them forever, but she saw Nathan differently now. He'd matured. When she looked at him, she saw a man. Good strong lines in his face and a hard, firm body.

Instead of a carefree student, she saw a caring and very competent surgeon. Instead of worrying about football games and spirit rallies, he held people's lives in his hand. Instead of pressing her for kisses and jumping right into bed, he held back so that she wouldn't be pressured into something she wasn't ready for.

He was very different from the college guy she remembered. The only thing that hadn't changed was that he was still so handsome he took her breath away. And he still held her heart in his hands.

LAURA STOOD in the living room of Nathan's home and tried to take in everything at once.

The antique brass chandelier, the polished mahogany of the carved tables and the secretary in the corner that must have dated back to at least the early 1800s.

"You've come a long way from the dorm, Dr. Nathan Duncan."

"I took my time getting here, but I like it. One day it may even be paid for."

"It's not at all what I expected."

"Did you think I'd still have beanbag chairs and TV trays?"

"No, but I pictured you in something angular and modern, with stark white walls and sleek leather recliners."

"I did, too, while I struggled though my residency. Then I moved to New Orleans and got caught up in the history of the city and decided I wanted to be part of it."

"How old is this house?"

"It was built in the early 1900s by a sugar plantation owner for his daughter and her family. He had five daughters and he built each of them a shotgun double, all within six blocks of each other."

"A shotgun double?"

"The style got its name from the fact that if

you opened the front and back doors, you could shoot off a shotgun and the bullet would go in the front door and out the back. This one is a double because it has two sides built along that same plan. This one has a hallway that was added during a later remodeling project. Most shotgun doubles don't. The foundation, floors and outside walls are all part of the original structure. They built them to last back then."

"The furniture seems to fit with the style. Did you choose it yourself?"

"I had some help from an interior decorator I dated for a while—until I found out she was ripping me off. Then I started making estate auctions and bidding on pieces myself. I got burned a few times, but I learned from my mistakes."

Yet another side of Nathan that she'd never even glimpsed during the short time they'd dated. "You are a fascinating man. How did you ever stay single all these years?"

"Med school. Internships. Residencies. Need I say more?"

"I guess that would keep you busy and out of trouble."

"School and poverty. What about you and

Grover? That was the name of the guy you left
Georgetown to marry, wasn't it?''

"That was his name."

"Did you two ever marry?"

"No. It didn't work out between us." It still
amazed her that he'd bought that story. She'd
been so in love with Nathan she'd hardly
known other men existed. There was no way
a Christmas vacation could have changed that,
though it had changed her life forever.

"Let me show you to your bedroom," he
said, leading the way to the back of the house.
"You should try to rest after lunch. It's easy
to overdo it the first day out of the hospital."

"I haven't done anything yet."

"And you're not supposed to. I'll get lunch
for you before I leave and I'll cook dinner tonight."

"I could get used to this."

He stopped and leaned against the door-
frame, letting his gaze meet hers. "If you do,
you can always stay."

The tension swelled between them, filled the
room and seemed to raise the temperature by
several degrees. It would be easy to slip into
his arms and make promises neither of them

could keep. Easy, but wrong. She'd built her world around him once and then walked away when she had no other choice. She couldn't do it again, not to either of them.

"I appreciate the offer," she said, and left it at that.

"Yeah." He shrugged and motioned toward the room just past the doorway where he was standing. "This is your room. It's small, but it has all the comforts I could squeeze in here."

She stepped inside and felt as she'd walked back in time. The bed was a four-poster with an awning of green silk shantung rippling over dark wood. A handmade quilt in shades of brown, green and gold covered the bed. The chest in the corner was hand-carved, the rug a rich wool Persian. A bouquet of fall flowers graced the top of a bedside table inlaid with pearl.

"I feel as if I'm in a museum."

"Then trash the place a bit. It's supposed to be livable. I'll go put lunch on the table. It's just soup and salad from the deli. I hope that's okay."

"I've been on hospital food for a week. Cardboard would be an improvement."

"That's what I like—a woman who's easy to please."

"I will need to go back to my apartment and get my things eventually."

"I've already taken care of that."

"How?"

"I called your landlady and told her someone would be by to pick up your clothes later today."

"What someone?"

"One of my former patients has a moving business. This will be a piece of cake for him."

"But now my landlady and your former patient know where I'm staying."

"They may know where Jill Jacobs is staying, but they know nothing of Laura Blankenship."

"They will if Hampton shows up."

"Hampton probably gave up on finding you long ago and is involved with someone else."

Nathan's theory would probably be right when applied to ninety-nine percent of American men, but Hampton fit in that one percent who would hold on to his fury until he found satisfaction in revenge. He'd never forgive her for running away and he'd never stop looking for her—not until one of them was dead.

Nathan turned back the quilt and plumped the pillows on the bed. "I've been thinking about what you said last night. I know you can't risk calling Hampton, but what about his friend, the one who came on to you on the beach that day? Would he level with you if you called him, tell you what Hampton is doing and if he's still obsessed with finding you?"

"He would if he's had any more contact with Hampton."

"Then why don't we call him? If he gives you good news, you might be able to relax a bit. If he gives you bad news, you'll be no worse off than you are now."

"I suppose that would give me something more concrete to go on. When do you think we should call?"

"Now would be good. Do you know his number?"

"I can get it. He was staying with his brother when I left. If he's not still there, his brother would probably give me his current number and I know his brother wouldn't say anything to Hampton. He hated him, said he used Tim and never gave anything back."

Nathan handed her his cell phone. She punched in the number and waited.

"Hello."

"Is Tim Cotter in?"

"Who is this?"

"It's Laura Parker. I'm trying to reach Tim."

"Where the hell are you?"

"It doesn't matter. I just need to talk to Tim. Do you know how I can reach him?"

"We all thought that the two of you ran off together. That's what your husband's been telling everyone."

"Tim's not with me. I haven't seen him since I left Los Angeles."

"Well, no one around here's seen him, either. He's been gone since right after you left, just up and disappeared the way you did. If he's not with you then...."

She shivered, suddenly chilled to the bone. She broke the connection without saying goodbye. Her head dropped to Nathan's shoulder and when he put his arms around her she settled inside them, needing his touch and his warmth.

"Bad news?" Nathan asked as he stroked the back of her head and neck.

"No one's seen Tim since right after I left."

"Not even his brother?"

"No. Tim's dead. I know he's dead."

"You can't know that. You disappeared and you're fine."

"But Tim was trying to get back with his girlfriend. He had no reason to leave town. Hampton killed him."

"Is that what Tim's brother thinks?"

"He thought Tim was with me, but Hampton killed him. I know that he did. Someone always has to pay." Grief for Tim burned inside her and mingled with the neverending fear—fear for herself and for Nathan. If she was with him when Hampton caught up with her, he'd kill Nathan the same as he had killed Tim and Leopold.

She'd slept in the bed of a cold-blooded murderer, made love with him, carried his name. The thought of it made her sick to her stomach.

"I wish you weren't going back to the hospital today."

"I can stay."

"I can't ask you to do that. Your work is important."

"So are you. Friday afternoons are always

slow. I only have two appointments and Babs can reschedule them for one day next week."

"I warned you that I'm nothing but trouble."

"And still I want you here. I guess that says it all, Laura."

"Sweet, kind, strong Nathan." She wrapped her hands around his neck and kissed him. She hadn't planned it. If she'd thought about it, she'd never have done it, but now that she had, the need she'd worked so hard to keep tamped down exploded in a burst of passion.

Her life was in chaos, shrouded in danger. She had no right to do this to Nathan, no right to thrill to his kiss or to feel such raw, unbridled hunger for him.

She had no right to want him, but she did.

Finally, breathless and weak, she pulled away. "I didn't mean to do that."

"I'm glad you did. I've wanted to kiss you ever since that first day in the hospital when I realized that my gypsy woman was Laura Blankenship."

"We can't just take up where we left off fifteen years ago."

"No, but we can build on that. Even you

can't deny that the attraction is still there, not after that kiss.''

"I can't make any promises, Nathan.''

"I'm not asking for promises. All I want is a chance for us to see what we are together. I'm in no rush. I've waited fifteen years to feel this way again. I can wait a little longer to see it through.'' He led her to the bed and eased her down until her head rested on the pillow. "Now get some rest. I don't advise sexual excitement for my recovering patients.''

"Now you tell me.''

She closed her eyes and willed away the fear and dread, imagined Tim alive, imagined herself in Nathan's life and in his bed as she drifted off to sleep.

HAMPTON FELT a dizzying swell of excitement as he broke the connection with his expartner's wife in Dallas and punched in the number for Sam Bailey. Almost a year, and this was his first solid lead.

"Sam Bailey. What can I do for you?''

"Take a trip to New Orleans.''

"Is this Hampton Parker?''

"It is. I have a lead I want you to check out.'' He gave Sam the details and the names that had come from some stupid story on a cable news show.

"If this does turn out to be Laura, do you want me to confront her and try to bring her back to Los Angeles?"

"No. I'll take care of that myself. I just want to know where to find her."

"Gotcha."

"When can you leave?"

"As soon as I can get a flight. It costs more if I book at the last minute."

"Cost is no object. I want Laura found, the sooner the better."

"Any other instructions?"

"If there's a man in the picture, I want his name and address. And don't let anyone know who you are or that you have any connection to me."

When they finished the deal, Hampton poured himself a double whiskey, walked outside, slipped out of his robe and dived into the pool. Laura could have been here with him, could have had all of this. Now she'd have nothing. Not even her life.

CHAPTER FIVE

NATHAN'S STATEMENT about the first day home from the hospital being rough proved true on Friday night. Not only had she been tired, but Laura had experienced her first real pain since the surgery, a dull but persistent ache just above her left temple. Nathan had served her dinner in bed, fretted when she ate only a bite or two of his pasta and hovered over her until she'd fallen asleep with the aid of a pill he'd insisted she take.

There had been no repeat of the passion they'd shared at lunch, no energy left for stolen kisses, but Nathan had been sweet and compassionate, and that was the biggest turn-on of all. At least she felt that way this morning, waking to thoughts of him, the bright glare of sunlight streaming though her open curtains and the chirping of birds outside her window.

Nathan was probably stretched out in the

middle of his bed, sleeping soundly. The image fired her imagination. For all the time they'd spent together at Georgetown, their lovemaking had always been the frenzied fabric of young, impatient lovers. She'd never gotten to kiss him awake in the morning. Never shared breakfast in bed or made love with him when he was all groggy from a full night's sleep.

She hadn't done it then, and she didn't dare do it now. Every intimacy they shared would make it just that much more difficult to walk away when the time came. And lying here thinking about it was getting her nowhere. She stretched, then climbed out of bed and padded into the hall in her cotton jammies. Nathan's door was open. She peeked inside. The sheets were mussed and kicked back, but Nathan was nowhere to be seen.

A quick burst of panic skittered along her nerve endings. Anything unexpected always affected her that way, but she had to get past it. Precautions were necessary. Prudence was wise. But if she was going to give into unreasonable paranoia at every turn, she might as well be back in the house with Hampton where the only thing she could depend on was that disaster was never more than a heartbeat away.

The smell of coffee wafted down the hallway. She'd lost her taste for it after surgery, but it smelled good this morning. By the time she reached the kitchen, she could hear the sizzle of strips of bacon being plopped onto a hot griddle.

"A man who brings home the bacon and cooks it, too, is every woman's dream."

Nathan turned and flashed her a dazzling smile that showed all his nice white teeth. "Yep. Most mornings I have them lined up at the door fighting over who gets to come in first."

She didn't doubt it, not if he always looked as good as he did right now. His long, muscular legs and chin were sprinkled sparsely with dark hair, just enough to give him that masculine look. Alligators and bottles of Tabasco danced about his boxer shorts and his T-shirt advertised the challenge of running in the annual Crescent City Classic.

She ran a thumb along the hem of his boxers. "You have definitely acclimated to your surroundings."

"It's easy to acclimate to a place that always gives you a little lagniappe and the philosophy is *'Laissez le bon temps rouler.'*"

"Can you say that in English?"

"Guess I have acclimated. I thought that was English. Lagniappe means a little extra and the last saying means 'Let the good times roll.'"

"You always were a fun-loving sort of guy."

"Not always. I had a really bad Christmas once." He took a mug from the shelf, poured some coffee and handed it to her as if he hadn't just hit her with a pointed reminder that she'd been the one who'd walked out on their relationship the first time around.

He forked a slice of bacon and turned it over. "By the way, what ever happened to old Grover?"

Fifteen years ago the lie had seemed important. Today she had to wonder why she hadn't trusted Nathan with the truth. At any rate the lie had festered between them for too long.

"Grover married Mary Ellen Nichols, opened a string of car washes and had four sons. The last time I talked to Mary Ellen she'd just had her tubes tied.''

"Sounds like Grover must have gotten one of your special Christmas cards, too.''

She propped her backside against the counter so that she could make eye contact as they talked. "I made up the story about staying in Longview to marry Grover. He didn't even enter into the equation.''

"It would have been nice to have known that then. But if it wasn't Grover, it must have been me. Did our relationship frighten you that much?''

"It didn't frighten me at all. I was mad about you, but I couldn't return for the spring semester, and breaking everything off with you seemed the best solution for both of us.''

"You *couldn't* come back or you *chose* not to come back? There's a big difference.''

"The choices were never the same for me as they were for you. My family didn't have any extra money.''

"You had a full scholarship.''

"And I had four younger siblings. When I got home for Christmas vacation my mother gave me the bad news. She'd been diagnosed with cancer and given six months to live. They needed me at home.''

Nathan shut off the element under the bacon and took both of her hands in his. ''You never told me about your mother.''

''If I had, you would have felt sorry for me and never broken up. I didn't want a relationship based on pity.''

''Did it ever occur to you what your not wanting pity cost me?''

''I don't see how it could have cost you anything. The only change for you was that I was no longer in your life.''

''You say that like it was nothing. I nearly went crazy after I got that note saying you were marrying someone else. I flunked out that semester and almost lost my scholarship and my chance to become a doctor. I drank myself into a stupor at least five nights a week and even played around with drugs. An overdose nearly killed me one night and I just plain didn't give a damn.''

''I'm sorry, Nathan. I didn't know.''

''Because you didn't bother to find out. I could have been there for you, Laura. You could have been there for me. Instead you shut me out of your life.''

''I probably made a mistake, but there's no use dealing with the pain all over again. I can't undo my decision, and even if I could, it wouldn't change the way things are now.''

''How can you say that when you're doing the same thing again?''

''I'm not lying to you about Hampton. I've told you the complete truth.''

''But you're shutting me out. You can't stay with me because you're afraid for me. You think Hampton's too dangerous for me to handle so you'll face him on your on. You weren't even going to tell me who you were. You'd have just dropped into my life, then walked out again without ever letting me know you were there.''

''You make it sound as I have some selfish motive. Hampton will kill you if he finds out we've been together. I can't let that happen.''

''It's not yours to *let*. Hampton is a madman but you didn't create him.''

''You don't understand.''

''The hell I don't.'' He dropped her hands and paced the floor before stopping near the table that had already been set for two. "I've had to learn to accept the fact that I can't control the world. Some patients I can save. Some I can't. When I lose one it hurts, but if I let it destroy me, I won't be able to help the ones I could save."

"We're not the same. Our situations are not the same." Frustration tore at her control. "I shouldn't have come here."

"That's just the point, Laura. You should *always* have been here. Can't you feel how right we are together? I don't want to lose you again, not without giving us a chance."

"What kind of chance could we have? What kind of life could we make together when Hampton will always be out there, like a precariously balanced rock waiting to fall and kill us both?"

"So you're willing to just let the bastard win?"

"It's not what I want."

"What do you want, Laura? I guess it all comes down to what you want and how badly you want it."

"I want to give us a chance, Nathan. I want it as much as you do, but I don't want to force you to live in my fear."

"I wouldn't. We'd live together in love. But only if you can let me share your life—all of it. We're either together in everything or we're not together at all."

"You make the choice sound so simple."

"It is simple. If we're going to have a chance at having a relationship, then you'll have to stop running and you'll have to stop shutting me out."

It was simple to Nathan, but he was a rational man who lived in a rational world populated by rational people. He'd never witnessed the cold, cruel systematic destruction of everything that mattered to him. He'd never lived with Hampton Parker.

"Give us a chance, Laura. That's all I'm asking. Don't run."

"I'll try, Nathan. That's all I can promise."

"Then I guess I'll have to settle for that." He opened his arms and she stepped inside them. He kissed her and the ugly, dark world she'd escaped from seemed to fade away. In his arms, lost in his kiss, she could *almost* believe they had a chance.

LAURA HAD MOVED to New Orleans in June and spent the sweltering summer months outdoors in the heat performing gardening chores for several of the homes near Tulane University—the only work she'd been able to find without references or a social security number.

She'd wondered then why anyone endured the climate. But now it was fall, and she understood. Sunday afternoon was especially magnificent, mid-eighties and not a cloud in the sky. Being with Nathan made it infinitely more wonderful. The whole weekend had been like a dream, the ones she used to have before she'd married Hampton and moved into the Twilight Zone where dreams always dissolved into nightmares.

Nathan had a knack for making life fun and easy. They'd talked and laughed for hours, caught up on each other's lives, shared memories from the unforgettable semester when they'd been together at Georgetown University, and even moved into the realms of politics and religion. They'd played a few serious games of chess and dissolved into giggles and a popcorn-tossing fight over a game of You Don't Know Jack. They'd taken advantage of his courtyard to cook out and to dance in the moonlight to hauntingly sweet instrumentals played on his stereo.

The only thing they hadn't done was talk of the future…and make love. She knew Nathan was trying not to put pressure on her, not to force her to move too fast. She loved him for that, and his methods were working. She'd begun to relax a little, had felt the knots of fear that she'd lived with constantly over the past few years begin to loosen.

She stretched out on the pool recliner and reached for the bottle of red toenail polish she'd brought outside with her. Before she'd finished the first toe, Nathan had climbed out of the pool where he'd been swimming laps and joined her.

"I think you're exerting yourself," he said, standing over her and giving his body a brisk rub with a fluffy beach towel. "You could probably use some help with that."

"Handling this heavy brush and spreading the polish over the entire nail is a bit tiring."

"I thought so."

"You brain surgeons are so perceptive."

"And we're good with our hands."

"So I've heard. If you didn't have that nasty habit of cutting chunks of women's hair while they were asleep, you'd really be terrific."

"Hey, we never cut women's hair. We have an assistant do that." He reached up and ruffled hers. "Besides you look cute like that."

"I look like a punk rocker."

"Now you're talking fantasy stuff." He pulled up a chair so that he could get to her toes. He dipped the brush into the polish and wiped it against the inside of the bottle to avoid drips before he smeared the bright red color across the nail of her big toe.

"You've done this before."

"You didn't think you were messing with a novice, did you?"

"Apparently not."

The feel of his hand on her foot was unbelievably erotic. It had been a year since she'd been with a man. She hadn't missed it until Nathan had come along. Sex with Hampton had lost its passion and joy long before she'd left. The tension and strain of never knowing when one of his blowups would occur had robbed her of any kind of spontaneity and enjoyment, killed any kind of sexual urges she might have had before they had a chance to begin.

"This is wonderful."

Nathan held up her foot to admire his handiwork. "I do have a nice touch with a brush, don't I?"

"A very nice touch, but that's not what I was talking about."

"So what's wonderful?"

"Just being together like this. Talking, teasing, being myself." She clapped her hands together as the reality of what she'd said hit her full force. "That's it. I'm just being myself. For the first time in years, I'm not worried about everything I say and everything I do. I don't have to guard every emotion with you. Even if you're not happy with me, even when we were talking about why I left you years ago, you didn't fly into a rage and try to destroy some part of me that made me whole and secure."

"I'd never willingly hurt you, Laura."

"I know that. That's why this works, why the knots inside me are beginning to unravel. I know it sounds crazy, that being one's self seems such a natural thing, but a bad relationship robs you of that.''

''It doesn't sound crazy at all. The only crazy part was that you ever let this lunatic convince you that you were anything but terrific.''

''I was probably easy prey. While everyone else my age was dating and building relationships, I was being the breadwinner and mother to my younger siblings. When my youngest sister graduated from high school, I was finally ready to start my own life and who should come along but suave, sophisticated Hampton Parker, rich restaurateur, to sweep me off my feet?''

''You could have called me.''

''After fifteen years. I never dreamed you'd still be single.''

''I wouldn't have been if I'd ever found anyone who could replace the sweet, vivacious Laura Blankenship.'' He finished the last toenail, screwed the top back on the bottle and set it under the edge of the recliner. ''That's why I can't lose you again, Laura. I'll wait however long it takes until you're ready to try love again—as long as I don't have to let you walk out of my life."

"I'm not the person I was back at Georgetown, Nathan. I've been through too much. Life has changed me."

"Life changes all of us. Some good. Some bad. But deep inside you're the same. Sweet. Gentle. Witty. Intelligent. All the things I loved about you fifteen years ago are still there. They might get swallowed up by the fear occasionally, but they're still there, along with that nebulous attraction that makes a man love one woman out of all the women in his life."

He stood, took her hands and pulled her up and into his arms. "I love you, Laura. I always have and no matter what happens between us, I always will. God help me, but I always will."

And then his lips met hers and she melted into his kiss. The years that had separated them slipped away along with her fear-induced inhibitions. The old thrill returned, sizzled through her and turned her insides to something hot and flowing and tempestuous.

She kissed him again and again, parted her lips and felt his tongue slip between them. Desire swelled inside her and she pressed closer, feeling the hardness of him against her warm skin. She was breathless from his kisses, but she couldn't pull away. The feelings were familiar and brand-new all at once and she simply couldn't get enough of him.

Finally he withdrew and held her at arm's length. His breathing seemed strained and the bulge in his bathing suit was obvious. She wanted him, his touch, his lips, all of him. The passion was so strong, she could barely contain it.

"Can I make love, Nathan?"

He looked puzzled.

"I mean, can I make love this soon after the operation? You said you didn't advise sex for your patients."

"I don't. I usually suggest they wait two weeks to a month."

"You said I've made a remarkable recovery."

"You have. Making love itself wouldn't hurt you, as long as it wasn't wild and boisterous."

"Then be gentle with me."

"Are you sure?"

His asking did for her heart what his kisses

had done for her body—filled her with warmth and a deliciously decadent hunger that begged to be satisfied.

"I'm sure."

She didn't say the rest, that she still couldn't make promises. But right now her heart was overflowing and making love with Nathan seemed more right than anything she'd done in all her life. And if she didn't do it now, she might never have the chance.

He kissed her again, a soft, moist kiss that reached deep inside her and pushed back the jagged edges of fear.

"I'm very, very sure," she whispered as he lifted her in his arms and carried her to his bed.

LAURA WAS STILL bathing in the afterglow of the lovemaking hours later, dangling her feet in the swimming pool while Nathan grilled shrimp and sausage. She'd already made the salad, the one thing he'd let her do all weekend that even slightly resembled work.

"You have a nice lifestyle, Dr. Duncan."

"It's looking up."

"What would you be doing this afternoon if I wasn't here?"

"Probably this. I usually don't plan social activities for Sunday evening. I like to unwind and get ready for the next hectic week."

"The type of surgery you do must be mentally and physically demanding."

"Actually the surgery is the easy part. It's intricate, tedious and exhausting, but it's what I was trained to do and I love it. The hard part is dealing with the fact that I can't save everyone. It's heartbreaking to look a person or their family in the face and explain that they're not going to make it. You know it from the other side, when you found out that your mother had only months to live."

"Life is precious, isn't it?"

"And too often wasted on things that don't really matter."

"What matters to you, Nathan?"

"My work. Friends. My family, though I don't get to see them nearly often enough."

"I know. I've missed my brothers and sisters terribly this year. I've let them know I'm safe, but I don't dare contact them. I'm afraid that even a phone call might somehow be traced. I don't put anything beyond the limits Hampton would go to in order to find me."

"Hampton Parker will soon be a nonentity in your life."

"I'd love to know how that's going to come about."

"I'm not sure yet, but we'll find a way. Divorcing him will be a start."

Nathan was a brilliant man, but if he thought Hampton would be persuaded to let go of her because of a piece of paper that said he should, he still had a lot to learn.

"I didn't finish my list," he said when he caught her look of disbelief.

"Let's hear it."

"And the number one thing that matters to me is…" He gave a drumroll with the handle of his spatula against the metal grilling pit. "You."

"I like your list."

"Then you're going to love my shrimp. And they're ready. Do you want to eat outside?"

"Definitely. It's a beautiful evening. I'll get the salad."

"Can't have my patient working. I'll get what we need from the house. If you need a task, light the candle. There's a lighter in that basket next to the beach towels."

"Okay, I can handle lighting your fire."

"You already did that."

Once the candle was glowing, she went back to her spot by the edge of the pool. It was nearly twilight and the temperature had dropped a couple of degrees. The end of the day. The end of the perfect weekend. Apprehension flickered inside her. Things had been too perfect. Something would go wrong soon.

No, that's the way it was with Hampton. She had to let go of those fears.

Only she never would, not as long as he was out there, still looking for her.

The phone rang.

"Can you get that?" Nathan called from the kitchen. "It could be the hospital paging me."

She picked up the portable phone he'd left by the grill. "Hello."

There was nothing but silence on the line. Terror hit in waves and her legs refused to hold her up. She staggered to a chair. "Hello."

No answer, but someone was there. She could hear their breathing. A few seconds later she heard the harsh click as the caller broke the connection. The phone slipped from her shaking hands.

Nathan pushed the door open, both hands full. "Who was it?"

"My husband."

Nathan's face began to blur. Her eyes were open, but the world disappeared and she sank into the depths of blackness.

CHAPTER SIX

THE PLASTIC PLATES, napkins and silverware dropped from Nathan's hands and clattered against the patio floor as he rushed to catch Laura before she crumpled and fell. He'd never hated a man before, but he hated Hampton Parker. He couldn't even imagine the kind of beast who'd terrorize his own wife so badly that just a phone call from him could petrify her to the point where she blacked out.

He gathered her in his arms, carried her inside the house and gingerly lay her on the upholstered sofa. She was stirring by the time he got her head propped up on a couple of throw pillows. "You're safe, Laura. You're right here with me, and you're safe."

She met his gaze, her eyes wide and glazed with terror, then she jerked to a sitting position and scanned the room. "How did I get in here?"

"You fainted. Does that happen often?"

"It's never happened before." She shuddered and cradled her head in her hands. "I have to leave now. Hampton knows I'm here, and he's coming."

"Did he say that?"

"No, he didn't say anything."

"Nothing?"

She shook her head. "Not a word, but it was him. I know it was."

"You mean the person who was on the line just hung up without speaking?"

"Not the person, Nathan. Hampton."

He took her hands in his. They were as cold as ice and she'd started trembling. "You need to take it easy for a few minutes. Lie back down and relax. I'm going to get you a blanket."

Delusional and paranoid. The words flashed across his mind as he retrieved a blanket from the linen closet. Flashed over and over as if someone had turned on a neon sign. Was it possible that Laura actually was suffering from psychiatric problems as the missing person's report claimed, that she'd imagined all the things she'd blamed on Hampton? Was Nathan just so enamored of her that he'd ignored all the signs?

Her fear seemed so compelling, so formidable that it was hard to believe it had no tenable basis, yet this time it had been triggered by no more than a hang-up, which more likely had been a wrong number than a case of stalking.

His mind considered the possibility briefly and then rejected it. Laura was running on fear and frazzled nerves, but it was not unwarranted. Hampton had done a number on her, made her life a living hell and convinced her that he'd see her dead before he'd let her leave him. She believed him capable of murder, and Nathan couldn't be certain that wasn't a valid assessment, not after the things she'd told him. At the very least, Hampton was a dangerous psychotic.

By the time Nathan returned to the living room, Laura was nowhere in sight. "Laura?" No answer. He raced to the guest room and found her cramming her clothing into her oversize duffel. "What are you doing?"

She kept packing.

He grabbed her hand and tugged her away

from the luggage and into his arms. "You have to stop this, Laura. You can't go through life running at every bump in the night."

"It wasn't a bump. It was a phone call."

"A hang-up. That doesn't mean it was Hampton."

"It wasn't just a hang-up. He stayed on the line for a few seconds, no doubt loving the frustration and panic in my voice, when all I could hear was his breathing. He used to do that to me all the time. Call to make sure I was home, especially late at night when he was at the restaurant or out of town on business."

Nathan ground his teeth, biting back the curses that sprang to his lips at the thought of Laura being tormented by a man who must have been tutored by the devil himself. "I have caller ID on the phone in my home office. Walk down there with me. We'll check the phone number of the caller."

She looked at the duffel, as if she hated to leave it. "Do you have a gun in the house?"

"There's one in the bedroom."

"Is it loaded?"

"No."

"Go load it, Nathan. I know you think I'm

overreacting, but if Hampton finds us together, he'll kill both of us. Our only chance will be if we have a weapon.''

He stroked the back of her head as he held her, trying to calm her and get her to think rationally. ''Has Hampton ever killed anyone before? And don't count Tim because you don't even know that he's dead.''

''Not that I know of, but I saw him try to kill Tim for making a drunken pass at me. If he thinks we're living together, that we've been lovers, he won't stop until we're dead.''

''You've been separated for almost a year.''

''A year for his fury to breed and fester. He doesn't forget and move on like most people. He broods and plans his vengeance until the time is right.''

''I'll load the gun.'' He still didn't think they had a thing to worry about, but he'd do whatever it took to placate Laura until he could convince her not to run. Legitimate fear or baseless paranoia, it didn't matter. He just wanted to take care of her—and love her.

They walked hand in hand to his bedroom. Reaching behind a leather-bound copy of Moby Dick, he removed the semiautomatic, then retrieved the shells from the top drawer of his bureau. He'd bought the gun a year ago when several of the doctors in town had had their homes broken into by a teenage gang searching for drugs. The thugs responsible had been arrested shortly after that, and he'd never even loaded the .38.

He was uncomfortable loading it now, especially with Laura watching as he dropped each bullet into the chamber. The action seemed to make the danger more real, as if they were actually expecting a killer to come bounding through the door while they ate or slept.

"If Hampton shows up, we'll be ready for him," he said, keeping his voice low and as calm as possible. "Now let's go check the phone."

She only nodded. He wrapped an arm around her waist and led her to the small room he used for his office. It had been added on by the last owners and was little more than a glorified closet, but it housed his computer, printer, fax machine and a couple of file cabinets.

He checked the number of the last incoming

call. It was a local number, and the message read "caller not recognized."

Laura read it at the same time he did. She wasn't trembling anymore, though. Her body was stiff, her expression blank, and he knew she was planning her next move. If he didn't do something quick, she was going to walk out of his life.

He punched redial and let the phone ring a dozen times before he hung up. "No answer."

"Let it go, Nathan. Let *me* go. You have a perfect life and you deserve it. You made the right decisions. I made the wrong ones and I have to live with them."

"My life is only perfect if you're in it, and I'm not about to concede defeat to a madman. I have a connection with the N.O.P.D. He can check out the phone number and tell us exactly where the call originated." He flipped through his organizer until he found Dutch's pager number. Time seemed to pass in slow motion until Nathan got him on the phone.

"I've got a little problem here, Dutch."

"Something else involving Hampton Parker."

"Indirectly. I had a caller who hung up a

few minutes ago. My caller ID didn't identify him, and when I dialed the number a few minutes later, no one answered.''

''Have you had problems with this before.''

''No, but there are some extenuating circumstances now. I'd appreciate if you could check it out for me.''

''No trouble. I'll get back to you on the double, Doc.''

''I appreciate that.''

He gave Dutch the number and thanked him in advance. Laura was standing by the window, looking out into the gathering darkness when he finished the conversation and hung up the phone. Her arms were wrapped tightly around her chest, as if she were literally holding herself together.

''Are you hungry?'' he asked. ''We still have shrimp and salad.''

''I couldn't possibly eat now. I'm sorry, Nathan.''

''Nothing to be sorry for. The food will keep. Let's go back to the kitchen and have a glass of wine.'' Hopefully that would relax her.

''I'd rather have a cup of tea.''

''Then tea it is.''

Tea and a heaping helping of her past. He almost wished Hampton Parker was in town, that this could all come to a head and that they could deal with it and get past it. Laura couldn't go on living in paralyzing fear. Neither the mind nor the body could take that kind of stress indefinitely without breaking. Something had to be done. He just wished he knew what that something was.

LAURA SAT at the table sipping her tea while Nathan took the call from his cop friend. She knew from listening to Nathan's end of the conversation that the information was inconclusive. The rush of adrenaline she'd felt while packing her duffel had passed, leaving her stomach churning and her arms and legs leaden.

She couldn't imagine why she'd fainted when she'd never fainted before. Maybe it was the extremes of emotion she'd encountered over the past few days. The joy of being with Nathan compared with the horror of Hampton. Or perhaps the operation had left her system weakened and her body had momentarily closed down.

"The call was made from a pay phone at the hospital," Nathan said, once he'd broken the connection. "It could have been anyone."

"If it was someone on staff, wouldn't they have used a hospital phone or their own cellular phone?"

"Probably, but sometimes family members of patients call to ask me questions that they don't want the patient to overhear. One of them could have easily stepped out of the patient's room and made a call on the pay phone."

"The caller didn't ask any questions."

"Something could have interrupted the call or the person could have changed his mind. Dutch suggested that he try to reach Hampton in Los Angeles. He has access to a phone that won't allow the person called to see the number even if he owns a sophisticated caller ID machine. If Hampton's still there, we'll know he's not the one who made the call from the hospital."

"Does Dutch have the name of the restaurant?"

"He has all the information. I had him check the files for Laura Blankenship when I first suspected who you were. He got a copy of the missing person's report Hampton filed.''

"One more person who knows that I'm actually Laura Blankenship.''

"I only told Dutch that I'd heard from you. I didn't tell him you were the woman the newspapers called Jill Jacobs.'' He walked over, stood behind her chair and massaged her shoulders with his strong hands. "You've lived with a monster, Laura. It's no wonder you're afraid to trust anyone, but the world is filled with good, honest people. Dutch is one of them.''

And so was Nathan. And he loved her. The pure wonder of it seeped inside her and touched the frayed edges of her brutalized heart. "I don't know what I've done to deserve you.''

"Love doesn't have anything to do with deserving. Love just is.''

Maybe it had been the miracle of love that had brought her to New Orleans even though she had no way of knowing that Nathan was here. Maybe they were meant to be together, meant to be here at this moment in time.

Maybe it was an omen that she'd be able to fully escape Hampton.

Or maybe she was only fooling herself into believing the impossible. The shrill ring of the phone broke into her thoughts. Her blood ran cold as Nathan took the call. They'd have the verdict soon. If they couldn't reach Hampton in Los Angeles, she'd have to go with her instincts.

Love for Nathan would make her run.

"Terrific news, Dutch. That's exactly what I wanted to hear." He turned to her as he ended the call. "Hampton is at his restaurant tonight overseeing a business dinner that some corporate head is throwing for a hundred guests. From the music in the background, Dutch concludes that it is a swinging affair."

The news sank in slowly.

"I thought you'd be exuberant," Nathan said, tugging her to her feet.

"I am. I'm just slow to trust good news. There hasn't been a lot of it over the past few years."

"That's all going to change, Laura. Nothing but good news from now on. You'll see."

He kissed her with sweet, gentle passion and

a silky warmth crept inside her. The words *I love you,* were on the tip of her tongue, but she didn't dare say them out loud. Love was frightening and way too risky. Hampton had destroyed everything she loved over the past few years, had almost destroyed her in the process. She couldn't let his poison touch Nathan.

"What do you say we eat that shrimp now?" Nathan said. "Hampton Parker is clear across the country and immersed in his own life. You have nothing to fear."

Nathan had always been a dreamer.

HAMPTON HURRIED down the concourse at LAX. The airport wasn't crowded this time of night, but it had seemed to take forever to get through security and he had no time to waste if he was going to catch the red-eye to New Orleans. New Orleans and Laura with some doctor she'd picked up. Met him last week and living at his house this week. No telling how many men she'd slept with since she ran away from home.

A cheap slut. That's all she'd ever been, but he'd loved her all the same. He'd given her everything. A luxurious house. Fancy clothes.

A generous allowance. And all she'd ever done was vex him and make him do things he hadn't wanted to do.

Now she'd really made him angry. This time he wouldn't forgive her. There would be no more lessons, no more punishment. This time she had to die, she and her lover.

The anger that had seethed and smoldered inside him for the past year had erupted at Bailey's call, exploded in a fiery torrent of hate that consumed him. It was too late for pity. Too late for absolution. Too late for Laura and Dr. Nathan Duncan. It was just too damn late.

LAURA WALKED through the house, hating the quiet now that Nathan had left to go to the hospital. She loved being with him, hearing his voice, having breakfast across the table from him. Loved touching him, kissing him and sleeping in his bed last night.

It was almost as if the years that had separated them had slipped away and they had never been apart. When she was with him, she felt younger, more vibrant, so happy that for brief periods of time, she could almost forget the uncertainty and fright that had been her constant companions since marrying Hampton.

Then something would happen such as the phone call last night or just a sound or a thought, and the icy fear would come rushing back in and she was back in the nightmare again. Nathan thought all it would take was time, but he was wrong. All the time in the world wouldn't eliminate the terror as long as Hampton Parker was out there somewhere, waiting to get his revenge.

Pouring another cup of coffee, she took it and the newspaper and walked back to the bedroom. The covers were still mussed where she and Nathan had slept, and she felt a warm tingle of desire dance along her nerve endings. They hadn't made love again last night. Nathan didn't want her to overdo it so soon after the surgery, but they had kissed and cuddled and touched, and it had satisfied her soul if not her ravenous hunger to make love with him.

She walked to the sliding glass doors that opened onto the back courtyard and the pool. The sun was glaringly bright and already she could feel the heat seeping through the wide doors. She pushed the door open and stepped outside. The pool recliner beckoned, and she sat down to soak up a few rays before she went in for her shower.

She closed her eyes and slipped into the fantasy of what it would be like to be Mrs. Nathan Duncan, to have a whole lifetime of loving him.

Her muscles grew tight and her nerves strained as a chilling shudder ripped thorough the fantasy. It was as if Hampton had invaded her mind and turned the images black. His presence was so real she could almost hear his breathing and smell the cloying sweetness of his cologne.

"Looks like you've made yourself right at home."

The voice sliced into her like a jagged-edged knife and her heart plunged to her stomach. She opened her eyes and stared into the frigid, terrifying wrath of her estranged husband.

"You've betrayed me, Laura, and you've broken my heart. It was not a smart thing to do. Now we're going to go inside so we won't disturb the neighbors."

His eyes were like stones, cold and hard and

black as night. He'd come to kill her, the way she always knew he would.

"YOU'RE A POPULAR GUY," Carl Madison said when he crossed paths with Nathan.

"How's that?"

"Some guy was at the hospital yesterday looking for you and your gypsy woman."

"Who was it?"

"He didn't say. I'm sure it was a reporter. There's nothing else going on now, so they'll milk that story for all it's worth."

"What time was that?"

"He cornered me about three when I came up to check on one of my patients who was experiencing complications. But he was still here at five when I left. I saw him talking to that cute redheaded nurse in ICU."

"And he didn't give his name?"

"No. I didn't ask, but he didn't offer it."

Carl was probably right. The man had probably been a reporter and the timing fit for him to have made the phone call, the one that had gotten Laura so upset last night. Still, Nathan didn't like the fact that some man who hadn't identified himself had been hanging around asking questions about him and Laura.

Maybe Laura's paranoia was contagious.

There was nothing to worry about. Hampton was in Los Angeles, probably in another relationship by now. Men like that weren't happy unless they had someone to push around.

His cell phone rang just as he reached the door of his first patient. "Hello."

"This is Dutch. I've got some news for you, Dr. Duncan, and I don't think you're going to like it."

HAMPTON PUSHED Laura through the back door and into Nathan's bedroom, twisting her arm painfully behind her back. "Too bad your boyfriend isn't still here. I'd hoped to finish you both off at once."

"He's not my boyfriend."

"No, just your bed partner. Do you think I can't look at this bed and tell you slept in it together? It smells of you, Laura. Your fragrance is all through the house, but it's especially here where you slicked the sheets last night."

"It's not what you think, Hampton. Nathan is an old friend, and he's just letting me stay here until I recover from the operation. Do what you want to with me, but leave him out of it. He hasn't touched me and he doesn't even know about you."

"You do think I'm a fool, don't you? The guy has touched you, the same way a hundred other guys probably have since you ran out on me. A woman who'd get it on with her husband's best friend will sleep with anyone."

"It was never like that. Tim was drunk and lost his head."

"Yeah, well he's lost a lot more than that now."

"What did you do to him?"

"The same thing I'm going to do to you, sweetheart. Punish you for your sins."

"Oh, God, you didn't kill Tim?"

"Ah, but I did. The same as I'll kill you, but first we're going to redecorate the doctor's house for him, give him a little surprise when he comes home, before he gets the real shocker." Holding her with his right hand, he picked up a crystal vase from Nathan's dresser with his left and hurled it across the room. The vase shattered and sent a shower of glass all over the room.

Her stomach tied itself in sickening knots. The games had begun and by the time they ended, she'd be dead—unless she could find some way to stop him. He dragged her to the window, tightened his grip around the fabric of the drapes and yanked it from the wall, pulling a large chunk of plaster down, as well.

"Please, Hampton. Don't do this. Nathan hasn't done anything to you." Even as she said it, she knew it didn't matter. Leopold hadn't done anything to him, either. He just destroyed for the fun of it, to satisfy some sick need.

"You really like this doctor guy, don't you, Laura? Then I just might keep you alive a while longer so that you can watch me kill him. I want to see the look in your eyes when blood comes spurting out of his head. I'll blow the brains right out of the brain surgeon, and you can watch, my pretty one."

Her stomach churned. She was going to be sick. She doubled over then straightened again. She had to be strong, had to think clearly and find a way out of this. If not for her then for Nathan.

Hampton picked up the phone and thrust it into her hand. "Call your boyfriend, Laura. Tell him you need him and that you want him to come home."

"No."

He twisted her arm until she cried in pain. "I said call him."

"No." He shoved her against the wall, and she heard her the loud clunk of her head hitting the window facing. "You can batter me all you want, but I'm not calling Nathan."

"You'll call."

"No, I won't. You're going to kill me anyway, but I don't have to help you destroy the one innocent person in all of this. He's as good as you are evil, and I won't help you kill him."

Hampton's face turned a bright red. He was losing control now, the way he had when he'd caught her in Tim's arms. The thick blue veins in his neck and forehead emerged and his face was contorted into the hideous expression of a madman.

He tore the phone from the wall and slammed it into her shoulder, then shoved her to the floor. Pain shot down her arm and up her neck to the base of her skull. She was dizzy and weak, but she managed to slide from his grasp and throw herself at his knees. She hit hard and he went down.

In that split second, she dived to the bookcase and yanked the pistol from its hiding place. She pointed it at him, her finger poised on the trigger.

"You won't shoot me, Laura."

"I will. If you take one step toward me, I'll kill you, Hampton. I will. The world will be a better place without you."

He lunged toward her. She pulled the trigger. The sound was deafening, but Hampton kept right on coming. He slammed into her and knocked her into the glass door, sending the pistol careening through the air like a missile. His hands were on her throat now, cutting off her supply of oxygen. There was no blood on him, no gaping wounds. Somehow the shot had missed its mark. It would be her who died.

Just as she started to lose consciousness, he released his hold on her neck. "It's a lovely day for a swim, and you know how I love my daily swim. I bet the doctor doesn't even have to heat his pool in the fall and winter. One of the benefits of living in the deep south. But I guess you know all about the benefits, don't you? You've been cashing in."

He pushed her out the door and she staggered toward the pool, barely staying upright.

But still she didn't give up. There had to be some way to fight back.

She never got the chance. He picked her up and tossed her into the water, then jumped in after her. She tried to swim away, but he caught her legs and pulled her to him, then ducked her head beneath the surface.

She tried to fight, but her arms flailed uselessly. He was too strong. She held her breath as long as she could, then felt the choking water burn her nose and her lungs. Hampton's fingers were tangled in her hair as he pushed her lower and lower into the depths of the cool, blue water. It didn't hurt anymore. She was just going to float away.

I love you, Nathan. I love you so very, very much. And for the first time in a long time, she knew that everything was going to be all right. Hampton wouldn't hurt her anymore.

CHAPTER SEVEN

NATHAN SKIDDED to a stop in his driveway just as a police car came flying up behind him. He ran to the front door, unlocked it and pushed inside. "Laura. Lauuuura!" Panic rode every frayed nerve in his body as he raced through the house. When he stepped into the bedroom, his heart started to pound against the walls of his chest. The gun was on the floor. He picked it up, then stopped dead in his tracks.

The pool was in full view. A man was crawling from the water. Laura's body was below the surface, sinking steadily, her blond hair flowing like a halo above her head. Hampton Parker had made good on his threat.

Something snapped inside Nathan as he watched his dreams sink toward the bottom of a pool of blue water. He aimed the gun at Hampton's head just as Dutch rounded the side of the house.

"Don't do it, buddy. The scum's not worth it."

Hampton saw them and took off at a run. Nathan dropped the gun and dove into the water. Even before he reached the surface with Laura, he knew there was still a pulse, faint, but it was there. He lay her down on the patio and started CPR, working steadily as he prayed for all he was worth.

Laura spit up a mouthful of water and opened her eyes, her dark, beautiful, mesmerizing eyes. "Yes, baby. Yes!" He kept at it, working with her until her breathing was steady and her pulse had returned to near normal. Then he cradled in his arms and rocked her back and forth, his own eyes moist and burning. He had come so close to losing her.

Dutch and two other cops walked up with Hampton Parker sporting nice metal handcuffs between them. "Is Laura all right?" Dutch asked.

"She will be."

Laura nodded and pushed a wet clump of hair from her forehead. "Thanks to you guys. Hampton had planned to leave me dead."

"Yeah, we had to run the murderous scumbag down, but we got him."

"I owe you more than I can ever repay, Dutch," Nathan said. "If you hadn't double-checked and found out that Hampton was on that early-morning flight, I would never have been home in time to save Laura."

"A good cop's gotta go with instinct. I kept thinking about that call last night and wondered if Hampton might have someone doing his legwork for him. Turns out he did. A dirty little private investigator who'll do anything for anybody for a buck."

Laura choked again, spit up more water, then resettled in Nathan's arms. "You might want to know that Hampton confessed to murdering his friend Tim Cotter before you got here," she said.

Her voice was hoarse and still a little shaky and the knowledge of how close he'd come to losing her hit Nathan all over again.

"The L.A. police will be glad to hear that," Dutch said, "and it will also make certain our man Hampton gets to spend a long, long time in jail, hopefully for the rest of his natural life."

Hampton glared at Laura, hate and fury glazing his eyes. "Too bad I didn't kill you, Laura Blankenship. You were never what you seemed and the doctor will find that out for himself all too soon."

"I'll get him out of here," Dutch said. "You guys need an ambulance?"

"No. I'm taking Laura to the hospital to get her checked over, but I'll drive her."

"Thought you might."

The cops left with Hampton in tow.

Laura breathed a huge sigh of relief. "Looks like you saved my life again, Doctor. Do you know what that means?"

"I hope it means you're mine."

"Forever and always." She wrapped her arms around his neck. "The nightmares are finally over, and all my dreams have come true. I'm not afraid to say it now. I love you, Dr. Nathan Duncan."

"And I love you. It's taken me fifteen years to get you back, and I am never letting you go again."

"Is that a promise?"

"No. It's a miracle."

She snuggled contentedly in his arms. "Better than a miracle, Nathan. It's love."

PRIMAL FEAR

Caroline Burnes

PROLOGUE

LONG HAIR rode the crest of the swell, looking almost like a tangle of seaweed in the pink-stained light of dawn. The gentle wave broke, and the body bumped the sandy bottom of the shore.

Down the beach an older woman bent to pick up a shell. She stood up and dropped it in the bucket she carried on her arm. Shading her eyes with her hand, she looked south, out toward the barrier islands. Her grandsons were planning an excursion to one of the islands, where they could play in the more forceful surf of the Gulf of Mexico. The harbor was too tame for the twin twelve-year-olds. She smiled as she thought about their total enjoyment of the beach.

In the east the sun lifted from the horizon. It was going to be another scorcher. Another shell caught her eye, and she started forward, then stopped, her attention riveted to something on the beach nearly fifty yards in front of her.

Another gentle swell washed in, lifting the body and depositing it farther up on the shore. The dark hair fanned across the sand.

The woman began to run, dropping the bucket of shells she'd been collecting. As she drew closer to the body, she slowed. Her hand went to her mouth to stifle the scream as she saw the terrible damage that had been done by sharp, vicious teeth. For a long moment she stared at the body, and then she turned away and ran, retracing her steps to the beach cottage she owned on Pirate Harbor and the telephone that would bring the sheriff.

CHAPTER ONE

LIBBY PHILLIPS stared at the sandy stretch of beach. It looked innocent enough. Now.

Only yesterday, it had been the scene of a gruesome discovery by a Pirate Harbor resident. This was where the body of the latest shark attack victim, Isabelle Mathis, had been discovered by Anna Krane, a woman who was still suffering from the shock of her horrible find.

"This is the third shark attack of the season." Sheriff William Darring repeated what he'd told her on the phone. "Folks around here are spooked. The idea of being eaten by a shark is ruining the tourist business, and Charlotte County depends on the trade that swimmers and divers bring to the area. That's why the county decided to put together the money to hire you. We need some answers, Dr. Phillips, and we need them soon."

"Yes," Libby said. She studied the shore-line, finally turning her attention to the expensive homes that fronted the harbor. She shifted her gaze to the south where a row of barrier islands separated the Gulf of Mexico from Charlotte Harbor. "Are you sure the attack took place *in* the harbor?"

"Dr. Phillips, I'm not sure of anything anymore. We've never had a summer this bad." Darring tilted his hat back on his head.

"Were the first two victims attacked in the harbor?" Libby pressed the issue. She'd spent the majority of her adulthood studying the habits of sharks, and what she was learning at Charlotte Harbor, Florida, didn't correspond with typical shark behavior. Normally, sharks didn't venture into harbors.

"No, ma'am. The other bodies were both in the Gulf, on the other side of the barrier islands. One diver and one swimmer."

"The latest victim, Ms. Mathis, was she diving?" Perhaps the attack had occurred in the gulf and the body had somehow drifted into the quiet harbor waters.

The sheriff hesitated. "It's difficult to say. She was a diver, but she wasn't wearing any gear when she washed up, so it could have come loose from the body. She's one of those treasure hunters off the *Sea Lady*. She was Chad Watson's partner.''

Libby's eyebrows lifted. "*The* Chad Watson. The guy who found the *Liberty* and the *Nina?*''

"That's him. He's been lurking around Gasparilla Island. Been out there for several weeks and acts like he's on a secret mission and—'' He broke off abruptly.

Libby looked up at the sheriff. He was a tall, well-built man. His eyes were hidden behind sunglasses, and she couldn't tell what he was thinking, but his tone and word choice hinted at a personal dislike of Watson. She could understand it. Watson had been the star of several television adventure shows. He'd found a fortune in artifacts and jewels on a Civil War ship, the *Liberty*, and he'd won the hearts of scientists and historians when he'd found the watery grave of the Portuguese galleon, the *Nina*. He also projected a tremendous ego and an attitude that let everyone know he lived in the fast lane and liked it that way. Fast boats, fast cars and beautiful women were accoutrements of his lifestyle.

She stared at the sheriff's sunglasses and wished she had a pair for herself. The Florida sun was bright. Even with the recent shark attacks, the harbor was still filled with small sailboats, Jet Skis and swimmers. On the far side of the barrier islands there were more sunworshipers on the beach and in the aqua water of the Gulf.

"What did the autopsy report on the victim show?" Libby asked.

"The report isn't complete. I sent you everything I have, so far. The coroner said the shark wasn't a monster, just average-size. He's taking the cautious route and treating this like a simple shark attack." He shook his head. "The body had been in the water several days before it washed ashore. But I still can't figure why a shark would come into the harbor to feed. Sharks belong in the open water, not the bay."

Libby didn't respond, but she wondered if there was more to Isabelle Mathis's death. Perhaps the sheriff would rather have a human killer than killer sharks. It would be less devastating to the gulf-based economy of the county.

But Libby knew the treachery of a shark. After her brother's death ten years before from a shark attack—also in Florida waters—Libby had learned never to take the behavior of nature's most perfect predators for granted. Though there were normal patterns of behavior, she never believed it was predictable. Not surprisingly, her specialty was sharks that were abnormal in their actions.

"Who reported Ms. Mathis missing?" she asked.

William Darring took a deep breath. "No one. That's one of the things that bother me."

"But you said the body had been in the water several days?" Libby didn't bother to hide her shock. Surely someone had missed the woman.

"It's a troubling point," Darring said. "You'd think someone who worked with her would have noticed she wasn't showing up. I've questioned Watson and his crew, but they weren't what I'd call cooperative. In fact, Watson was downright uncooperative. Not to mention that he and Ms. Mathis had an argument in a bar just before she disappeared.''

Libby felt a tingle of concern. "Are you implying that Ms. Mathis's death might have been something other than accidental?''

The sheriff took off his sunglasses, his gray eyes staring directly into hers. "I don't have enough evidence to say that. I can only repeat that it seems strange to me that no one noticed her absence.''

"Surely someone did.''

"Yes, I'm sure someone missed her. My question is why no one reported it,'' Darring clarified.

"Mr. Watson had no explanation?'' Libby couldn't imagine someone in the diving business not keeping tabs on all crew members.

"His exact words were until I had proof that foul play was involved in Ms. Mathis's death and an arrest warrant, he didn't have to talk to me.''

"That sounds just like something Chad Watson would say,'' Libby said. "He's incredibly arrogant.''

"Or guilty of something,'' Darring added.

The sound of a speedboat captured her attention, and Libby watched as a sleek pleasure craft shot toward them like an arrow. A man stood at the wheel.

The wind whipped his curly brown hair, and Libby found herself noticing how thick and alive it looked in the wind. His broad shoulders and muscles showed beneath the tight black T-shirt he wore.

"Speak of the devil," William said, "and he appears."

"Chad Watson." Libby muttered the name as she recognized him. He was far more handsome in person than he was on television. Handsome and self-possessed. He stood in the boat as if he owned the entire ocean. The look in his eyes spoke of self-confidence and ease. And arrogance.

"Any new discoveries, Sheriff?" Watson called out as he jumped from the boat and waded in the shallow water toward the shore.

"He won't answer my questions, but he expects me to answer his," William said under his breath to Libby. "We'll see about that." He addressed the next statement to Chad. "Running that fast in shallow water is dangerous. You'll hit a shoal and break your neck."

"Luck runs in my favor," Chad said with a grin. "Have you found out what happened to Isabelle?"

"I don't feel inclined to share my investigation with a man who may be my prime suspect," William replied, pulling his hat brim down.

Chad ignored the sheriff's comment and turned to Libby. "You must be the marine scientist they hired to study the shark attacks. Isabelle was the third attack. Do everyone a favor and convince the sheriff to close the beaches. Before other people are hurt."

Libby was curious. Chad Watson seemed to care about Isabelle Mathis, yet he hadn't bothered to report her missing—for several days. "I'm sorry about Ms. Mathis," she said. "I understand she was your partner."

"Yes, she was." Chad's face had gone cold and stony.

"What was she doing, Mr. Watson? It would help me if I knew where she was when she was attacked."

"I thought that was what Sheriff Darring was going to find out," Chad answered brusquely. "Isabelle didn't answer to me."

"I find it odd that Ms. Mathis, a professional diver, didn't tell anyone on your ship where she was going or what she planned that day. Diving alone is always dangerous."

"Hunting for treasure beneath an ocean is always dangerous. Isabelle knew that. She knew the risks. I don't keep my crew members on a leash."

Libby noted that Chad didn't contradict her presumption that Isabelle Mathis was diving by herself. She pressed harder. "You have no idea where Ms. Mathis was diving when she was attacked?"

"I understood you were a shark expert, I didn't realize you would be part of the sheriff's interrogation team." Chad's lazy smile almost hid his anger.

"I'm a marine scientist, and I do have a lot of questions."

"I'm sure you do. As do I." He turned his attention back to the sheriff. "A lot of questions and a lot of concerns. My advice to you is to close the beaches and get the tourists out of the way of danger."

"But, of course, you feel *you* should be allowed to continue diving, right?" the sheriff pointed out. "Forget it, Watson. If the beaches are closed, they'll be closed for everyone. Including you and your treasure-hunting team."

Chad stared at the sheriff with cold anger. "I don't believe we're in your jurisdiction. Let me know if you find out anything new about Isabelle's death." He turned away and began wading back through the water. He hopped over the side of the boat, weighed the anchor and took off.

William shook his head. "Watson's concern for his partner is heartbreaking, isn't it?"

Libby kept her gaze trained on the rapidly receding boat and the man standing at the wheel. "Is he actually on a hunt near here?"

"He's after something, but he's very secretive about what it is. He's refused to talk to any of the media, and he won't tell me a single thing about what he's hunting for."

"The Florida coast is ripe with treasures," Libby said, remembering the history of the region.

"Sunken treasures aren't my concern, but possible murder is. Isabelle Mathis was attacked by a shark, but there may be a lot more to the story than that. Watson doesn't like to answer questions, but when I get enough evidence, he's going to answer all of mine.''

THE SPEEDBOAT skimmed the shallow waters of the pass, and Chad at last found himself in the aqua waters of the Gulf. But his mind was on the woman who'd been examining the shore with Sheriff Darring. He'd heard a rumor that the sheriff was bringing in an expert on shark behavior. For some reason, Chad had expected a man. A pained grin crossed his face as he thought of Isabelle. She would have had his head on a platter for such a thought. More than once she'd accused him of being sexist, and maybe she'd been right. If she were still alive, he might even admit it to her. He'd admit just about anything if he could go back in time and change the course of events.

He slammed his fist into the steering wheel of the boat. ''Isabelle!'' He shouted her name, because there was no one to hear. ''You damn fool!'' He hit the steering wheel again.

He turned the craft toward a tiny dot on the horizon that he recognized as his floating laboratory. The *Sea Lady* was his home, as well as his office. While most of the crew were eager to get to shore after a few weeks on the water, Chad didn't care if he ever left the ship. Everything he needed was on the *Sea Lady*—or beneath the ocean waters on which she rode.

His thoughts drifted back to the woman on the shore. She was pretty enough, though she did everything she could to hide it. He thought of her baggy clothes and the naturally curly red hair that she wore pulled into a tight ponytail. He wondered what had drawn her to study the behavior of sharks. They weren't cute and cuddly, and they didn't inspire a lot of sympathy. In fact, after the last three attacks, almost everyone he met wanted to kill all sharks they saw.

He could only hope that Libby would be able to convince Sheriff Darring to do the right thing and close the beaches. *To the tourists.* He was far too close to realizing his goal to quit diving now, but it would certainly speed things up if he didn't have a gallery of amateur divers trying to follow his every move.

He pulled up to the *Sea Lady* and caught the rope that one of his crew members threw down to him. In a matter of moments the speedboat was secured to the side of the ship, and he was on deck.

Since Isabelle's death he'd halted all diving, but he was eager to resume—as long as he was doing the diving himself. They were so very close to finding the *Bella Siena*. Even at the possibility he felt his pulse increase. This would be his biggest find. The *Bella* was reputed to be the ship Ponce de Leon had sailed to Florida when he was searching for the fountain of youth.

In researching the ship and its subsequent disappearance, Chad had come to believe she was loaded with a wealth of treasures. Eager for the wonders of permanent youth, the Spanish queen had bestowed jewels and money on de Leon to use as bartering chips.

"Any information on Isabelle?" Alex, one of the crew members, asked, interrupting his thoughts.

"Nothing new," Chad said. "The shark specialist is in town."

"Who is it? Walter Clark?"

Chad shook his head. "Libby Phillips, Ph.D. An expert in shark behavior."

"Great," Alex said. "Maybe she can figure

out what's got the sharks on a rampage and straighten them out. When are we going back down?"

There was eagerness in the young man's voice, and Chad responded to it. "Soon. I promise. We just need to be sure that everyone is safe."

Alex laughed. "That's not the reputation you've cultivated, you know. Everyone believes you risk life and limb. Your own *and* your crews'."

Chad smiled. "An old fuddy-duddy doesn't make good television. The American audience loves a risk-taker, a gambler, a man who ruthlessly puts everything on the line." He frowned.

"Well, you've convinced everyone of that."

Chad nodded, his frown deepening. "I sure did, but it may have been a big mistake."

CHAPTER TWO

THE FIRST THING Libby did when she got to her hotel room was plug in her computer and do an immediate search on Chad Watson.

She found what she was looking for on her third try, and she stared at the photograph of the beautiful Isabelle Mathis. She had been a lovely woman, and had an impressive résumé of dives and adventures. Libby couldn't help but think that Isabelle was the perfect female counterpart for Chad. She'd been independently wealthy, divorced and free to pursue life with the same grit and verve that Chad displayed.

Chad had taken the raven-haired beauty as his partner only the year before, when preparations for his newest—and most secretive—treasure-hunting adventure had begun.

And now Isabelle was dead.

Libby stared at the picture of Isabelle a moment longer, then clicked off the Web site. Her job was to study the sharks, not Chad Watson. She hadn't been hired to probe the circumstances of Isabelle's death. That was Sheriff Darring's concern.

She picked up the reports on the three shark attacks and several additional accounts of shark sightings. The details were troubling. It was not uncommon for the predators to feed in a pack, but according to the notes, the sharks actually seemed to be organized, plotting strategies with one another. It was pre-attack bonding, as if the sharks had developed a sense of community.

There was nothing in any respected studies that indicated sharks would act as a group. They were notoriously independent loners who never rested. Relentless eating machines that moved forward through the water to survive. Predators who preyed on the weak and the injured.

Sharks were all of those things—they did not participate in orchestrated behavior. But that was exactly the behavior reported by witnesses in the first two shark attacks off the Charlotte County coast. According to the eyewitnesses, the victims had been nudged and bumped by one shark, while at least a dozen other sharks had swum in circular patterns...waiting. When the attack had occurred, it had been swift and the sharks had worked together.

Libby reread the report, studying the element of timing. If the reports were accurate, the sense of play that preceded the attack was extraordinary. It was almost as if the first shark had been playing with its victim, much as a dolphin plays with humans. Then the play had turned deadly.

That description troubled her because it brought to mind her brother's death ten years before. Though no one had believed the reports, eyewitnesses on the beach described exactly the same scenario: the choreographed movement of the sharks, the strategic attack, the swift death of her brother, Wes, as several sharks went after him at once.

The first two Pirate Harbor deaths were similar. With Isabelle Mathis's death, there were no witnesses.

Libby put the files aside and walked to the window that gave her a view of the water. Pirate Harbor was a peaceful place that defied its historic name. In the past, the Gulf Coast had been a favorite location for many of the more famous pirates, and there was no doubt that sunken treasure abounded on the ocean floor.

What was Chad Watson after?

The ringing of the telephone interrupted her thoughts. She picked up the receiver, surprised when a newspaper reporter identified himself as Gerald Forrest.

Libby did her best to dodge the reporter's questions. She hadn't anticipated the attention of the media, and she realized she'd been naive. The shark attacks had been on national television for days. Once the media realized that Isabelle was part of Chad Watson's treasure-hunting group, the attention would only increase. Libby knew she had to be careful not to panic the public, but still make them aware of the danger the shark attacks presented. It was a fine line to walk and one that required verbal agility.

"Is it true that Chad Watson and Isabelle Mathis were heard arguing the evening before she disappeared?" Forrest asked.

The reporter's unexpected question caught

Libby's full attention. "I'm not involved in the investigation into Ms. Mathis's death," she said firmly.

"Then there is an investigation? The sheriff doesn't believe it was an accident?" Gerald pressed.

Libby wanted to bite her tongue. "That wasn't what I meant to imply. I merely meant to say that my involvement in the attacks in Charlotte County is limited to the study of the sharks' behavior."

"But the sheriff does view Ms. Mathis's death with some suspicion?"

"You'll have to ask the sheriff." Libby was losing her patience.

"One of our sources said that Isabelle Mathis worked for Chad Watson, and that they were romantically involved."

"I can't comment on that because I have no knowledge of it," Libby said, trying to keep an edge out of her voice.

"Rumor has it that Chad Watson will benefit financially from Ms. Mathis's death. Is that true?"

"How would a woman's death benefit him?" Libby asked, then wished she hadn't.

"It seems Ms. Mathis funded this latest adventure, and that she was pressing Chad for results. Can you confirm that?"

"No." Libby decided to try one-word answers because she knew Forrest would twist whatever she said.

"Have you spoken to Chad Watson?"

"Yes," Libby said. "In fact, he seems capable of answering all of these questions himself. Wouldn't it be better for your story to go directly to the source?"

"He won't return my calls," the reporter said. "He's available to the networks, but not to us local guys."

"Pity," Libby said, not bothering to hide her sarcasm. "I have work to do. When I have something to report on my findings regarding the sharks, I'll issue a written statement to the media." She hung up.

When the telephone rang a second time, Libby considered not answering. On the fifth ring she picked up the receiver.

"We have a boat ready for you," the sheriff said. "I planned on going out with you, but I just got a call from the coroner."

"What did he find?" Libby asked. The reporter's questions had left her with some dark thoughts.

"He said there are wounds on Isabelle Mathis's body that aren't consistent with shark bites."

"What kind of wounds?" Libby asked.

"I don't want to say more right now. Until I have all the details. Damn, I suspected this all along."

Libby swallowed.

"I'm headed to the coroner's office now, and I should have more information when I get back. Just be careful out on the water. I could send a deputy with you if you'd like."

"No. No, thanks," Libby said quickly. "I work better alone." It was true, but she also needed time to think.

"Okay. The boat is the *Quicken*. She's small and easy to handle, but big enough to manage the gulf waves."

"I've spent most of my life on the water," Libby assured him. "I'll be fine."

"If you're not back in by dusk, I'll be looking for you, and that won't be a good thing," he warned with a light tone in his voice. "If what the coroner tells me is true, there's someone out there a lot more dangerous than a shark.''

''No search parties will be necessary,'' Libby promised, though it did make her feel better to know that if she should run into trouble, someone would notice she was missing.

CHAD SURFACED, momentarily blinded by the bright summer sun glinting on the water. He treaded water while he removed his diving mask and searched the horizon to get his bearings. Only twenty yards away, the speedboat bobbed in the water, waiting for him.

He was eager to get back to the *Sea Lady* and report his findings, even though he knew his crew would be angry because he'd gone diving alone without telling anyone. Sometimes risks had to be taken—as long as they were personal risks.

And this was one of those times when risk was going to pay off. Big time.

He'd found a multicolored site marker, submerged at thirty feet. Isabelle's marker. He'd picked up her trail, and this had to be the location she'd been diving when she'd been attacked by the sharks. Treading water, he wiped his eyes. Isabelle had been the most hard-headed woman he'd ever known. She'd been determined to find the *Bella Siena* on her own, to claim the glory of the find. It had been important to her that she prove herself as capable as any man. The irony was that every member of his crew had already felt that way about her.

He hauled himself over the side of the boat, removed his tanks and diving gear and studied the specially ordered blue, yellow and purple site marker of the *Sea Lady*. There wasn't a doubt in his mind that Isabelle had been setting the marker when she was attacked by the shark.

He held the tag in his hand, trying to piece together Isabelle's last hours. She'd left the *Sea Lady,* saying she was going into town for some shopping. She'd never returned. The launch she'd taken was still docked at the harbor. So how had she gotten out into the gulf waters without a boat? Not a single bit of it made sense. Instead of focusing his attention on the shore, where Isabelle was last seen alive, it seemed Sheriff Darring wanted to point the finger of blame at the crew of the *Sea Lady.* All of the crew members had been with

Chad for years. They were above suspicion, and when Darring had implied that Chad or one of his crew had wanted Isabelle dead, Chad had lost his cool. It wasn't the smartest thing he'd ever done, but Darring rubbed him the wrong way. The sheriff seemed to be looking for the easy way out of a real investigation.

Chad turned the boat's ignition, ready to head back to the *Sea Lady,* when he spotted a large ship east of Gasparilla Island. The ship was outfitted with winches and booms much like the *Sea Lady.* Chad knew instantly that another treasure hunter had invaded his waters.

His first impulse was to aim the speedboat right at the bigger ship and initiate a confrontation. His hand was on the throttle when he stopped and rethought his decision. There were half a dozen treasure hunters in the world with rigs as sophisticated as his, but he didn't recognize this one. It would be in his best interest to find out who his competition was, before he went at them head to head.

LIBBY CLEARED the narrow pass that gave access to the Gulf and found herself rocking on the beautiful aqua swells of some of the world's prettiest water. It had been a long time since she'd enjoyed Florida's natural glory. Although Wes's death had pushed her into marine science, it had also pushed her away from the Gulf where they'd both grown up. She'd spent the past ten years studying the grayer Atlantic. Only the unusual aspects of the most recent shark attacks—and the hefty fee that Charlotte County was paying—had brought her home.

She headed along the south shore of Gasparilla Island, paying close attention to the nautical chart the sheriff had left for her. There were two marks indicating where the shark attacks had taken place, both amazingly close to shore. Neither attack had occurred during the sharks' normal feeding times of dawn and dusk. The more she studied the Charlotte County attacks, the more concerned she became.

As she cruised along the shore, she passed areas of beach that were dense with sunbathers. Just off the shore, swimmers played in the surf. Fear had driven away many of the sun-and-sand worshipers, but not all of them.

Libby noticed a large ship running parallel

to the island and slowed to study it. She was named *Enterprise,* and Libby knew at first glance it was a treasure-hunting boat. She was surprised when a red-haired man on deck waved at her, signaling her to tie up and board. Curiosity made her comply.

"You must be Dr. Phillips," the man said, shaking her hand. "I'm Barry Klass. I just spoke with Sheriff Darring on the radio, and he told me to keep an eye out for you."

Libby didn't recognize Klass's name, but the field of treasure hunting was growing larger and larger. Treasure and fame were hard for a certain type of man to resist. Whatever was beneath the gulf waters must be a very rich prize.

"Mr. Klass," Libby said, withdrawing her hand, "are you looking for anything special?"

"In my business, we're always looking for something special," he replied, his blue eyes crinkling at the corners. "But, as to details, I'm afraid I can't give you any. I wouldn't want word to leak back to my competition," he said, laughing.

He was a friendly man with an easy manner,

and Libby found herself smiling at him. "Then you know Chad Watson is already here?"

"Ah, Mr. Watson. I do believe he's staked his claim to all the waters of the gulf." He pulled a mock frown. "He's going to view me as an interloper. The sheriff has warned me that he's a very…ambitious man. But so am I, when the prize is worth it. Of course, I'm brand-new to the business, but I thought this was a capital place to start."

Libby lifted her eyebrows. "I've never known two professionals to go after the same treasure. Whatever is down there must be extraordinary."

"Only time will tell," Barry answered easily. "But tell me about the sharks. The sheriff insisted that I talk with you. He's afraid there'll be more attacks, which will translate into more bad publicity for this area."

"Not to mention more dead bodies," Libby said quickly. She decided not to mention the autopsy findings on Isabelle. That was the sheriff's province.

Barry laughed. "Yes, not to mention that."

"The sheriff is considering closing the beaches."

"We're professionals, prepared to take our chances. But we do use every precaution. Have you found anything so far on the sharks?"

"Nothing conclusive. I really haven't gotten started yet. But I'm checking out the locations where the attacks occurred. I'm hoping the terrain will give me some explanation."

"And I'm sure you'll let Sheriff Darring know the instant you find anything."

"Yes, of course." Libby eased her way back to the side of the ship where the *Quicken* bobbed in the waves.

"It was a pleasure to meet you, Dr. Phillips," Klass said as he helped her down into her boat. "I'm sure we'll run across each other again."

Libby pushed away from the ship, started her motor and cut a wide circle around the *Enterprise* as she continued along the coastline. Barry Klass's appearance would undoubtedly anger Chad Watson.

CHAD LOWERED the binoculars. Of all the things he'd expected to see, it wasn't Dr. Libby Phillips aboard another treasure-hunting ship. He'd gotten just close enough to check out the ship's name. The *Enterprise*. It wouldn't take long to determine who his rival was. He didn't know how, but rumors about the *Bella Siena* were apparently leaking. He had a friend in the Miami Police Department who was very good at finding information, and before the day ended, Chad was determined to know the whole story behind the *Enterprise* and her owner.

He thought again of Isabelle and her concern that someone would find the *Bella Siena* before they did. He'd thought she was simply over-reacting. Now he was reconsidering.

A sudden chill touched him. Isabelle must have found concrete evidence of the *Bella Siena*—he was certain of it. Why else would she have kept her diving a secret? And now she was dead. Was it possible her death was something more than an unfortunate shark attack?

He put his boat in gear and headed out toward the *Sea Lady*. Perhaps there was more to the sudden arrival of Dr. Libby Phillips than met the naked eye.

CHAPTER THREE

LIBBY PUSHED her unruly red curls away from her face and turned into the early-morning breeze. It was not even seven o'clock, and the day was already hot and humid. The *Quicken* bobbed in the water, and she sipped from her thermos of iced tea, closing her eyes for a moment in an effort to relax the tension in her body.

She'd been scouting the water just off Gasparilla Island for sharks since daybreak. So far, she'd seen nothing, but her hopes were still high. She finished the cold drink and picked up her binoculars.

She was looking east into the rising sun, when she saw the first fin. It cut the water, then disappeared, leaving her to wonder if she'd imagined it, or if the sunlight on the water had played a trick on her. Then she saw it again. This time, there were at least eight fins. She held the binoculars on the sharks and followed their progress toward her.

Without warning, the sharks turned toward shore, heading into the shallow waters that were normally too turbulent for good hunting. Unless the intended meal was human.

The school of sharks continued parallel to the shore, at last turning again toward deep water.

Libby found that her breathing was shallow. The sharks' movements were exactly as the eyewitnesses had described. It was as if they were hunting in a pack. If she could film their actions, it would make interesting study for marine scientists all over the world. Further study might also provide some answers to the unusual shark attacks that had recently occurred.

She was lowering the binoculars when she heard the sound of another boat. Turning south, she lifted the glasses and caught a clear view of Chad Watson at the wheel of his speedboat. He was headed straight for her at breakneck speed. With the binoculars, she could clearly see the expression on his face, and it was absolute joy. He was a man who loved speed, danger and risk.

It took less than five minutes for Chad to arrive, and he cut his engine and coasted up beside her, a grin still on his face.

"Any new discoveries, Doctor?" he asked.

"I didn't realize I was working for you," Libby said tartly. "The sheriff would be interested in your *interest*, I'm sure."

"The sheriff is interested in *everything* about me. Haven't you noticed I'm the perfect scapegoat? No doubt he implied I hurt Isabelle. That doesn't surprise me. What does is that as a scientist, I thought you'd require a little evidence."

Libby felt the flush rise to her cheeks. He'd hammered her professionalism, and her sense of fair play.

"I've only had time to make a few observations. Nothing significant," Libby said, suddenly aware of the way he was staring at her. She'd unbuttoned the oversize white shirt she'd chosen to block the sun. Even though she wore a swimsuit beneath it, she felt exposed as his gaze roved down her body.

His tone changed abruptly. "My cook

packed a breakfast. Would you join me on the island? Unless, that is, you're afraid I'm some kind of killer.''

Libby hated the way he taunted her, and she was determined not to let him get away with it. ''The sheriff is waiting for me to return. The pressure is really on for me to come up with some explanation about the shark attacks. I'll talk with you for a while, but I can't take long.''

''Perfect,'' he said. ''I'd like to hear about the sharks, as I have some concerns for the safety of my crew.''

''Of course.'' It was ridiculous for Chad's presence to make her so uncomfortable.

''Follow me into the cove,'' Chad directed before he started his engine and led the way into the inlet.

The water was crystal-clear and inviting as Libby dropped anchor and eased herself over the side of the *Quicken,* following Chad's lead. The cool water came only to her waist, and the sandy bottom was firm and pleasant. Small fish swam around her ankles, darting left and right.

In a moment Chad was beside her, picnic

basket held high out of the water. He hadn't been fibbing about the picnic breakfast.

"I love to come out here early, before other people arrive," he said. "You know, there was an attempt to develop this island, but it was defeated, thank goodness."

Libby cast a sidelong glance at Chad. He seemed perfectly comfortable expressing a sentiment that she would never have attributed to him. He wore a faded blue T-shirt, and it took her a moment to recognize the familiar logo of the International Marine Life Fund.

"You belong to the IMLF?" she asked.

"For twenty years. Since I was fifteen," Chad answered, grinning at her surprise. "I know, you believe that my only goal in life is to raid the watery depths for riches. I enjoy the image of the modern-day pirate, but I'm not all that heartless."

"I didn't actually mean that the way it sounded," she explained, feeling a warm flush touch her cheeks. It had sounded as if she thought he might be more Bluebeard than Jacques Cousteau.

"My crew is always telling me that I've taken the role of bad boy-playboy too far." He took her arm as they waded through the gentle surf and made their way onto the sand. "But it is an act, Dr. Phillips. Just don't tell anyone. I wouldn't want to blow my cover."

"Your secret is safe with me," Libby assured him drolly.

Pointing toward a stand of pine trees, he started walking. "My favorite picnic site."

Libby had to stretch her legs to keep up with his stride. This was not the Chad Watson she'd met only the day before. This man had a sense of humor about himself.

"Sorry, I didn't think to bring a towel," Chad said as he sat down in the sand and leaned against one of the trees. "Maybe you should take off your shirt and sit on it," he suggested.

It was a perfectly sensible suggestion, but Libby found herself unwilling to do it. At thirty-three, she was in good shape. Even with her fair skin, she loved the beach and the water—as long as sunscreen was in good supply. But there was something about Chad that made her all too aware of her own body. It was as if his very aliveness was contagious, and her body responded.

Instead of taking off her shirt, she sank down in the sand beside him. He handed her a sausage biscuit wrapped in a napkin.

"I happen to have the best ship's cook in the world. Fresh biscuits every morning."

"Thanks." Libby hadn't realized how hungry she was. The water always picked up her appetite.

"What were you doing on Barry Klass's ship?"

Chad's question came out of the blue. Libby paused, the biscuit almost to her lips. "How did you know I was on the *Enterprise?*"

"I saw you. I wasn't spying on you, but I noticed the ship and when I was trying to read the name, I saw you."

It was a reasonable enough observation, but Libby still felt slightly uneasy. "Mr. Klass hailed me and invited me on board."

"Don't you find it strange that another hunter has shown up in these waters?" Chad bit into his breakfast, his gaze trained out to the gulf.

"I was going to ask you the same question. I thought once a hunter had staked out a location, it was a matter of courtesy that others stayed clear.''

''Yes, the rules of the game,'' Chad said. His brown gaze swung to hers. ''Yet he's here.'' He paused a beat. ''And so are you. Do you know him? I've checked around, and no one's ever heard of Barry Klass before.''

Libby took a bite of the biscuit. This encounter with Chad wasn't chance. He'd sought her out. That would teach her to underestimate the treasure hunter. ''I don't know him. I never met him until yesterday. And I'll tell you what he said, though I owe you nothing. He said he was new in the business of treasure hunting.''

''How did he end up here and what's he hunting for?''

Libby turned to face him. ''I don't know. That's the truth. I don't know what you're hunting, either, but I can only assume that whatever you think is below the gulf waters, it must be a very lucrative prize.''

''Did he tell you anything else?''

''Actually, nothing. He's a pleasant man and he's got an expensive ship. That's all I can tell you.'' She shrugged.

Chad's next move completely astounded

her. He reached across with a napkin and daubed at the corner of her mouth. "Grape jelly," he said, and then continued to eat his breakfast.

Libby took a deep breath. Chad was totally unpredictable. One minute he was grilling her and the next he was wiping her chin. "I have a question for you."

"Okay. Turnabout's fair play."

"What was Isabelle Mathis doing diving alone, and why didn't someone report her missing?" She forced herself to hold her gaze steady. She could see the question offended Chad. But when he answered, his voice was calm, gentle even.

"Isabelle had something to prove to herself. She was the most competitive person I've ever met. Honestly, she made me look lazy. She told me and the rest of the crew that she was going into Pirate Harbor to do some shopping. None of us realized she was going to attempt a dive. As to not reporting her absence, that's simply not true. Reginald went into town the first evening she didn't come back to the ship. We searched everywhere for her, but because her boat was still docked, we assumed she was on land somewhere."

Libby considered what he said. "Are you certain your employee filed a report with the sheriff?"

Chad frowned. "Reginald's a good man. He wouldn't lie about something like that."

"He said he went to the sheriff?" Libby pressed.

Chad's frown deepened. "He specifically said he'd talked to the authorities."

Libby's eyes widened as the truth hit her. "He must have talked to the local police chief. Pirate Harbor is small, but there is a local police force."

"And the sheriff's office is in Charlotte County, not Pirate Harbor."

Libby felt a smile touch her lips, and she was surprised to see how Chad responded to it. Impulsively, he reached out and pushed a curl of red hair from her cheek.

"Thanks, Libby. I have a little better understanding of why it seems Sheriff Darring has it in for me. If he thought I hadn't reported Isabelle's disappearance, it would give him reason to be suspicious of me. He was more than a little hostile when he first questioned me, but I guess I can see why now.''

''It would tend to make anyone suspicious,'' Libby agreed. For some reason she was tremendously relieved to discover that one of Chad's crewmen had reported Isabelle's disappearance. ''You should talk to Darring and clear this up.''

''I will,'' Chad promised. ''What are your plans for the afternoon?''

''I've got to begin to document the sharks,'' she said. ''I saw them this morning, just before you came up.''

''We've all noticed the odd behavior. I've never seen anything like them,'' Chad said. ''The way they swim around and play, they're more like dolphins than sharks—until they attack.''

''That was exactly what I was thinking.'' Libby wiped her hands on the clean napkin he held out to her.

''How did you come to be interested in sharks?'' Chad asked.

Libby started to give him the pat answer that she'd grown up on the gulf and it was just a natural career choice. Instead, she heard herself telling him the truth. "My brother was killed in a shark attack about ten years ago. I vowed then that I'd learn more about them. I believe if we can understand what motivates sharks, we can prevent these attacks."

"I'm sorry, Libby." Chad touched her hand, which rested lightly on her knee. "That must have been awful."

"It was," she said. "I was going to school. My original career choice was a pediatrician. But when Mom called and said Wes was dead, that he'd been attacked in the gulf by sharks, my life changed."

"Was your brother a diver?"

"Very accomplished. He was a SEAL. He trained in these waters." She looked out toward the gulf in an effort to combat the tears that began to fill her eyes.

"I'd like to help you find out what's happening with the sharks."

Libby gave Chad a curious look. "How?"

"I'm diving this afternoon. Why not come with me? I have some of the best underwater cameras."

Libby felt her pulse rate jump. Chad Watson was inviting her to dive with him and to let her use his equipment. "I'd love to do that," she said, but another thought stopped her. "Chad, it may be dangerous."

He nodded. "My entire crew is aware of the danger. But so far, none of them has been attacked."

"Except Isabelle," Libby pointed out.

"Yes, except Isabelle."

Libby remembered what the sheriff had told her about the wounds on Isabelle's body. She started to tell Chad but thought better of it. Best to let William Darring and Chad come to terms with each other in their own way.

"Will you come?" he asked.

"Are you sure I won't discover your secret mission?" she asked, daring to tease him.

"If you do, I'll simply have to make you walk the plank," Chad joked, laughing as he rose to his feet and offered her his hand.

"Under those conditions, I accept." Libby let him pull her to her feet.

"I'm glad," he said. "I want you to find out what's provoking those sharks."

Chad's hand was still holding hers when Libby felt something sharp stab into her foot.

It was only his strong support that kept her from falling down. The pain was intense.

"Hey," he said, grasping her elbow firmly. "What'd you step on?"

"I'm not sure." She eased back down into the sand and didn't object when he knelt beside her and lifted her foot.

"It's a piece of shell," he said, holding her heel firmly in one hand. "I need to pull it out, but it's going to hurt."

"Great," Libby said. Her foot was already throbbing, and she saw droplets of blood falling onto the white sand. "Go ahead."

Chad swiftly pulled out the piece of shell and then bent to examine the wound. "Looks like I got it all. Lucky for us we have the perfect healing agent of the sea only a few yards away."

"Yeah, lucky for *us*," Libby said. "You're not the one who's going to have to stick an open cut into salt water."

He laughed at her obvious discomfort. "I don't think the wound is life-threatening, but I do have a medic on the *Sea Lady*. I'll be glad to have him take a look."

"No thanks, I'm not going to die," Libby said, trying to rise to her feet.

Before she could even stand, Chad had swept her up into his arms. "It wouldn't be a good idea to get sand in the cut," he said as he started walking toward the surf.

"I can walk." Libby felt the strangest sensation creep over her body. At first she thought it was embarrassment at having to be carried, but as her breast brushed Chad's muscled chest, she had to admit that she found his touch exciting.

"Chad, really, I can walk." She felt a sudden need to put some distance between them.

"Easy," he replied, holding her as she squirmed. In a moment he was wading into the surf. "It'll only sting for a second." He held her tight as the water covered her legs.

"Chad." She found herself staring into his dark eyes.

"See, that wasn't so bad, was it?"

His smile was touched with tenderness, and it was almost Libby's undoing. She had one flashing moment of imagining his lips on hers. Self-preservation returned, and she put a hand on his chest, pushing him away slightly.

"I'm fine. You can put me in my boat."

"Your wish is my command," he said as he settled her in the *Quicken.* "Maybe we should put off our dive."

"Not on your life," Libby said quickly. "I'll get some diving shoes."

He grinned at her. "A woman with determination. My favorite kind." He waded to his boat. "See you about two," he called back.

CHAD GLANCED OVER his shoulder to catch a last look at Libby in her boat, headed toward Pirate Harbor. She was the most interesting woman he'd met in quite some time. There was something so vulnerable about her, yet she'd chosen to examine the world's most perfect predator. She had a unique combination of determination and sensitivity that made him want to know everything about her. And he realized, with a wry smile, that he'd been jealous when he'd seen her on Barry Klass's boat.

His mind full of thoughts of the coming afternoon, he was at the *Sea Lady* before he realized it. As soon as he was on board he sent word for Reginald, only to discover that the crewman had gone into town to refill the empty air tanks for the divers.

Suddenly inspired, Chad called the five remaining members of his crew together.

"Take the rest of the day off," he told them. "Go into town, have some fun and be back here no later than nine tomorrow morning. We're going to resume diving."

He watched the men's faces as they cheered. They were eager to go back to work. None of them seemed to blame him for what had happened to Isabelle. Truth be told, all of them had known her and had known that she did exactly what she wanted when she wanted. It had been the only bad aspect of their partnership. And the only thing they'd ever argued about.

But argue they had. Publicly, too. In fact, their last fight had been on land in a bar called the Yardarm. Isabelle had imbibed liberally, and when she'd announced to Chad and several of the crew that she was no longer going to dive with a team member, but planned to pursue the treasure alone—despite two savage shark attacks—Chad had argued with her. It had been their last conversation, and he regretted that it had held elements of hostility.

"Are you coming?"

His thoughts were interrupted as one of the crew paused beside him before boarding the speedboat with the intention of going ashore.

"I'll stay with the *Sea Lady*," Chad answered. "The rest of you have some fun."

CHAPTER FOUR

LIBBY WAS JUST stepping into the *Quicken* for her trip out to the *Sea Lady* when she heard someone calling her name.

She looked up to find Sheriff Darring striding toward her. Libby stepped from the boat back to the dock and waited for him.

"Headed back out to the gulf?" Darring asked. He glanced at the diving gear Libby had stowed in the bottom of the *Quicken*. "You're not diving alone are you?"

"No. Chad Watson is going down with me. He's letting me use one of his underwater cameras. I hope to get some footage of the sharks."

"Not a smart idea, unless you're using a dive cage," Darring warned, his face showing his displeasure. "Surely Watson has enough sense to realize the danger involved in such a dive. I don't have anything official on him, but let me just say plainly that I don't think this is a good idea."

Libby, too, had thought of the danger—from the sharks and from Chad. "I have to watch the sharks to be able to determine what's going on. I know there's a degree of risk, but I'm sure Mr. Watson will do everything possible to keep us safe," she said.

"I'm not so sure of that." Darring stepped close enough so that he could speak low. "The wounds on Isabelle Mathis's body were made with a knife. She was cut and then put into the water like bait."

The images that rose to Libby's mind were ugly. She turned away to hide her reaction. "Are you certain?" Her voice came out shaky.

"It looks as if she was stabbed to death first, and her killer was trying to get rid of her body."

Libby took a step back, her gaze darting down the pier. A tall man whom she recognized as Barry Klass, was walking toward them. He was watching her exchange with the sheriff with interest. "Have you told Chad about Isabelle being cut?" she asked.

"I suspect he already knows."

Libby licked her dry lips. William Darring was saying that he thought Chad had deliberately murdered his partner.

"If I were you, I'd cancel your appointment with Watson," the sheriff continued.

"Mr. Watson has no reason to do anything to me. I'm not involved in a murder investigation. I'm only interested in the sharks. Using his cameras will speed up my work," Libby said, unable to control the tremor in her voice.

"We'll find other equipment."

"Where?" she asked. "Those cameras cost a fortune. It might take weeks to find some we can rent or borrow."

Darring rubbed his jaw with his hand. "There has to be another way so you don't have to go out with Watson."

Libby took a deep breath. She was trying to juxtapose this new image of Chad with the one she had of him gently ministering to her foot. He didn't strike her as a stone-cold murderer who would kill his partner. It wasn't his nature. Or that's what she'd come to believe.

"I'm not certain Chad had anything to do with Isabelle's death. I intend to give him the benefit of the doubt," she said in a softer tone.

Klass was almost on top of them, and Libby didn't want him to overhear the conversation.

The sheriff turned and recognizing Klass, waved a hand in recognition. "Maybe Mr. Klass has some equipment you can use."

"What kind of equipment?" Barry asked as he grinned a hello at Libby.

"Underwater cameras," William said. "Libby wants to film the behavior of the sharks."

Barry's eyebrows lifted. "That would take some expensive equipment. I don't have my cameras on the ship yet, but they'll be coming in at the end of the week. You're welcome to use them when they arrive."

"I'll be fine," Libby said, sounding more certain than she felt.

"I'll keep an eye out for you," the sheriff promised.

"Thanks," she replied. "Now I need to get my gear together so I can meet Chad at two."

THE *SEA LADY'S* galley was easily the most impressive Libby had ever visited. Copper-bottomed pots gleamed from hooks, and the appliances were state-of-the-art.

Across the worktop counter, Chad held up a bottle of wine. "After we dive," he said.

Libby nodded. "Where is the rest of the crew?" She tried to make the question casual, but even she heard the strain in her voice. Chad heard it, too. He lifted his eyebrows.

"I sent them ashore for a break. Is that a problem?"

"No." She spoke too fast, and forced a smile. She was nervous. The details the sheriff had given her about Isabelle Mathis's death had made her jumpy where Chad was concerned. "I'm just eager to get in the water."

"Then let's go." He gave her a strange look as he led the way to the deck where two diving suits and gear were waiting. Libby had her own suit, but the one Chad offered was superior.

She slid into the wet suit, wondering if it had belonged to Isabelle. It was a chilling thought. A tingle danced along her spine, and she turned to find Chad looking at her with open interest. The minute he felt her gaze, he looked away.

"I'll work the camera," Chad said. "I've used it before, and it's a little awkward. If you see something you want filmed, just tap my shoulder and point me in the right direction.''

"Thanks.'' She glanced at the rolling gulf. There was no sign of any fins in the water. ''I hope we get something. Will we be diving from the ship or from another location?''

Chad considered. ''I'd like to continue with my hunt, if that's okay with you.''

"That's fine.'' Libby was surprised. She hadn't expected that Chad would trust her with any information about his hunt, much less the location.

"Load up,'' he said, indicating the speed-boat.

She took the passenger seat and settled back as Chad opened the throttle. They seemed to fly over the crests of the waves, hitting hard enough to send spray flying around them. It was exhilarating, and frightening. Those were conflicting emotions she'd come to expect from close contact with Chad Watson.

There seemed to be no rhyme or reason to the place he stopped the boat. The gulf rolled around them, and Libby had to wonder how he knew where to stop.

"This is it,'' he said.

She picked up her mask from the bottom of the boat, then felt Chad's hand on her wrist, holding her in place.

"What's wrong?" he asked. "Suddenly, you're afraid of me."

She found she couldn't look in his eyes. She didn't completely trust him, and he was smart enough to sense it.

"I'm just eager and a little apprehensive," she said, trying to bluff her way through it.

"Libby, we have to trust each other. In the water our lives could depend on it," he said.

It was a point well made. Divers had to trust each other. There were too many opportunities for disaster. She didn't say anything.

"I brought you here to help me hunt for a sunken ship, the *Bella Siena*." When she didn't respond, he continued. "She was Ponce de Leon's ship. It's rumored that she sank in these waters while loaded with treasures sent as bribes for the natives, who were supposed to reveal the location of the fountain of youth."

Libby couldn't help it, she was fascinated by what Chad was telling her. For a second her fear was blocked by avid curiosity. "Have you located the ship?"

"No, but I think Isabelle may have been very close on the day she was attacked by the shark."

Libby felt the emotion churning inside her. It was impossible to merge the man standing before her with a cold-blooded killer. Chad Watson was an ambitious man. And he was a man who liked living on the edge. But that didn't make him a killer.

"Libby, what's wrong?" He reached out and brushed one of her unruly curls off her cheek. "I know something's troubling you."

"Isabelle wasn't killed by a shark. At least that's not all of it. Someone cut her and threw her into the water. She was already dead."

She saw the horror cross his face, quickly replaced by anger. "Who told you that?"

"Sheriff Darring. The coroner's report came in."

"Isabelle was murdered." His hands were clenched at his sides. "Who would do such a thing?"

"Who stands to gain financially?" Libby asked carefully. For a moment she thought she'd made the biggest mistake of her life. Chad turned to her with a look so furious she almost stepped back.

"That's what Darring is saying? That I hurt Isabelle over money?"

Libby lifted her chin. "He's not saying that, but the implication is certainly clear."

"It's a damn lie!"

Libby felt the tension in her body ease. Chad's denial of hurting Isabelle was so passionate, she knew it was real. "Who would want to hurt her?"

"That's a very good question," he said. The limitations of the speedboat didn't allow for pacing, but she could see that he needed action. He turned to her, his face suddenly open. "How long has Barry Klass been in the area?"

"I don't really know," Libby said. "I saw him yesterday, but…" She hesitated. "I saw him again this morning. He came up while I was talking with the sheriff."

"Very convenient, if I do say so," Chad fumed. "Who is this Klass? He suddenly appears with a ship that cost close to a million dollars and no one has ever heard of him before."

Libby shook her head. "He shouldn't be that hard to check out. Most treasure hunters are well documented on the Web. Your fans keep tabs on everything you do."

"He should be, but he isn't. Trust me, I've had a professional doing the checking."

"There's a lot of information about you on the Web. Perhaps that's how Klass learned where you were hunting."

"I've thought of that possibility. Of course, I'm not the only one who knows about the sunken ship. The *Bella Siena* is a real prize. The treasure could be a large fortune. And the acclaim of finding her is worth a lot. It was Isabelle who convinced me to take up the hunt. She was so positive she could pinpoint the location of the ship."

"How could she be so sure?" Libby asked.

"She was very secretive about her techniques." He rubbed his forehead with a thumb. "It was part of her appeal as a partner. She wanted everyone to believe she had some kind of mystical ability. That she could divine the location of the *Bella Siena*. I was always amused by her game."

"But you didn't believe it?"

Chad's laugh was both bitter and sad. "No. Isabelle wasn't a psychic or a witch. She was just a very determined woman who enjoyed games."

"Is it possible she was working with someone else?" Libby hated to raise the issue.

"Someone who double-crossed her and killed her?" Chad asked, jumping to the same possibility.

"No one knew she was out diving the day she was killed. At least no one on your boat," she pointed out. "Yet someone had to take her out to the gulf if her boat was docked."

Chad's face was grim. "You could be right. It's a real coincidence that Barry Klass shows up right after Isabelle died. He's violating the accepted rules of the business. But I don't want to point the finger of blame at him until we have solid evidence. Unfortunately, I know how that feels and it isn't pleasant. But if I find out he hurt Isabelle—" He broke off without finishing.

Libby reached across the boat and touched his hand. "I'm sorry, Chad. I know how painful this must be."

"Isabelle was more than a partner, she was

a friend. We had a unique partnership—competitors yet working for the same team. It was truly great. And now I find out someone killed her.'' His eyes burned with anger.

"I'll do whatever I can to help you find out who did this,'' she promised. "I came here to study the sharks, but it seems the two things are interwoven.''

"And we will find out,'' Chad vowed. "If Isabelle was murdered, and it's looking more and more that way, whoever did it is going to be caught and punished.'' He handed her a pair of fins. "Let's document these sharks. Then we need to go into town and ask some questions.''

THE SUBMERGED MARKER bobbed eerily in the water, and Chad swam toward it, leading the way for Libby. He turned back to make sure she was following and was struck once again by her graceful beauty. She was so completely unaware of her loveliness. With her red hair streaming out behind her, and her slender legs gently kicking, she was like an underwater goddess. Maybe, when Isabelle's death was resolved, he'd tell Libby how he saw her.

Once they reached the marker, Chad made

the calculations that he and Isabelle had agreed upon a few days before her death. He checked his watch and swam west. After five minutes, he began a descent.

Libby stayed right behind him, just slightly to the right. She had no trouble keeping up. The deeper they went, the darker the water got, until he had to slow considerably. If only he'd had a chance to talk to Isabelle, he might have an idea of the depth she'd reached. And if she'd actually found anything.

A swift movement in the water ahead caught his attention. Stopping, he reached back and caught Libby's elbow, just as the large, pointed body swept by him.

Shark.

It had cruised by him so closely that he could see one small eye and the open mouth that revealed a row of razor-sharp teeth.

Even though he'd spent years swimming in waters known to contain sharks, he'd never felt such a chill. He lifted the camera and began filming. He felt Libby's tap on his shoulder and swung left. There were four more sharks.

Using very slow gestures, she indicated that they were to remain still.

He complied, and in a moment the sharks swam past them, moving on. This was the behavior he'd come to expect of sharks—they didn't attack unless provoked or someone was injured. He glanced at Libby and saw her nod.

The relief was sweet, and he motioned they should proceed down.

She nodded agreement, and he led the way, alert now, but also eager. The water was dark, and he used the high-beamed light to scan the area in front of him. He almost missed the multicolored marker that swayed eerily. As soon as he saw it, though, he felt adrenaline rush through his body. Isabelle had been in this exact spot! He signaled Libby to follow the rope connected to the marker and they started the slow descent into the darkness.

Chad tried to calm the beating of his heart, but he knew that at the end of the line, he'd find the treasure that he'd spent endless months searching for. He felt Libby's fingers grasp his fin and tug, and then he saw it. The *Bella Siena* loomed out of the murky water in front of him.

Libby came up beside him and gestured excitedly. Together, they swam toward the hulk of the once proud ship that rested against the sandy bottom of the gulf, her main mast a broken stump.

Libby flipped on the light she carried, and they moved around the ship, finally stopping beneath the planks that bore the barely discernable name of the ship: *Bella Siena.* Chad ran his hand over the letters. It was almost impossible to believe. Isabelle had found the ship, and now she wasn't alive to enjoy her success.

A new rush of anger made him vow that someone would pay for her senseless death.

When he turned to Libby, he saw concern on her face and knew that she understood what he was feeling. He reached out to her and she took his hand. Together, they began to explore the exterior of the ship.

Chad didn't want to go inside the vessel without the rest of his crew. The old ship had weathered nearly three centuries beneath the salt water, but there was no guarantee that she wouldn't shift and trap Libby and himself. It was safer to wait until he had additional help in case of an accident. He turned the camera on again, and slowly began to swim around the ship.

Twenty minutes later, Chad had documented

the exterior of the boat from all angles. He was ready to surface. Tomorrow he'd have his crew down at the ship as soon as it was light enough to dive.

He was about to turn off the camera again when he felt a chill. Turning around slowly, he saw the dark shape headed straight at him. Beside him, Libby froze. She, too, saw the shark.

He shifted so that he was directly in front of Libby and in the shark's path. Surely the creature would veer away. He kept his movements to a minimum. When he felt Libby lift the camera from the strap on his belt, he didn't budge. She'd remembered what he'd forgotten.

The shark continued toward them, fast yet unhurried. It wasn't going to turn away. It was going to bump him. And then? He lifted the powerful halogen light and aimed it into the shark's eyes. Momentarily blinded, the shark veered away.

He felt Libby's touch on his arm and turned. Some ten yards away, five other sharks swam by. They circled Libby and himself, waiting. It was one of the most chilling things Chad had ever seen. Though he'd heard the eyewitness accounts of the most recent attacks, he'd assumed that the reports were hysterical. Except he was now looking at it with his own eyes.

Libby grasped his arm, and she gently used her flippers to begin the ascent. He grabbed her calf and held her. Now wasn't a good time to begin swimming. Sharks were attracted to movement. It would be best to stay put and wait for them to swim away.

Libby shrugged her shoulders and pointed to her watch. He realized then that they had no choice but to surface. They were very close to using all the air in the tanks.

CHAPTER FIVE

LIBBY BROKE THE SURFACE, feeling at once a sense of relief and renewed terror. She'd have to use more leg action to make it to the boat. She could only hope it wouldn't attract the sharks.

Chad surfaced beside her, and they began to slowly swim toward the speedboat. Although it was only fifty yards away, it was the longest swim Libby could ever remember making.

With each thrust of her flipper, Libby expected to feel sharp teeth tear into her leg. But even as she searched in all directions around her, she could find no sign of the sharks. It was almost as if she'd imagined them. Beside her, Chad was also scanning the water's surface for a telltale fin.

"Whatever happens, don't stop swimming," he instructed her.

When they reached the boat, Chad boosted

her up and over the side. He quickly followed. It wasn't until she was sitting in the bottom of the boat that Libby realized how afraid she'd been. Her body began to shake uncontrollably, and Chad helped her remove her tanks and wet suit, then pulled her into his arms.

"It's okay," he whispered over and over. "We're safe now."

"They were waiting there for us," she said, knowing that even as she spoke she sounded crazy. Sharks didn't plot out attacks. They didn't protect treasure ships. But these had. Or so it seemed.

"There's an explanation for all of this," he reassured her.

Libby felt the sun on her legs, the gentle rocking of the boat, and slowly she began to calm down. When she took a deep breath and allowed herself to relax in Chad's strong embrace, she could feel the tension slowly leave him.

"I'm fine," she replied, closing her eyes. "Really."

"I know," he said against her hair. "We're both okay."

For several minutes, they remained sitting in

the boat. At last, Chad stirred. "Let's get back to the *Sea Lady*. I want to take a look at some of that footage we took."

Libby pulled herself together. She wasn't ready to leave Chad's arms, but he was right, it was time to move. She, too, wanted to study the video they'd made. While she was primarily interested in the behavior of the sharks, she was also fascinated by the find of the *Bella Siena*. Chad had accomplished his mission. It was only a matter of time until his crew began to search the vessel for treasure.

"Are you going to leave a marker?" Libby asked.

He shook his head. "No. Nothing more than what Isabelle left already."

"How did you know where to begin searching?" she asked.

"Isabelle and I had already worked out the basic location. We'd plotted our target area, so I knew where to begin looking. I found her marker, but I didn't have time to go down and hunt more."

"So Isabelle found the *Bella Siena?*" Libby couldn't help the sadness that came with the statement. She hadn't known Isabelle, but apparently, the find would have been enormously important to her.

"I believe she did," he said. He signaled Libby to take the passenger seat as he checked the controls in preparation for leaving. "And I believe she was putting in that marker when she was killed. Someone must have caught her, tried to make her talk, and when she wouldn't, they killed her."

As chilling as the words were, they weren't unexpected. "And who do you think killed her?"

"Remember the question you asked me? Who stands to gain financially?" He waited for Libby's nod. "The first person who comes to mind is Barry Klass. There's no other professional around here looking for treasure. It's more than coincidence that Klass appears on the scene just when Isabelle is found dead. I just want to know who the hell he really is."

Libby couldn't argue with Chad's reasoning. As far as it went. His assumption was that Isabelle was killed while diving. But no diving gear had been found on the body. "Are you sure Isabelle was diving when she was killed?" she asked.

"I've done my own checking, but I never thought someone had hurt Isabelle until today. What I found out was that she docked at Pirate Harbor, went into the Beachcomber for lunch, then disappeared. I assumed she'd gone diving because her body was found *in* the water."

"In the harbor," Libby emphasized. "Which had me greatly concerned that the sharks had come into brackish water to feed. But since we know she was murdered, that puts an entirely new twist on it." As gruesome as Isabelle's murder was, it did seem to rule out sharks in the harbor. In fact, it seemed to indicate that someone had physically put Isabelle's body in the harbor water. Perhaps to cover up the location of the actual murder.

"We've been trying to find the *Bella Siena* for eight months," Chad said, his voice rueful. "Now the discovery is tainted by Isabelle's death. She wanted this so much. Whoever killed her is going to pay."

He started the engine and put the boat in gear. In seconds they were flying across the water to the *Sea Lady*. As soon as they'd boarded and changed into dry clothes, Chad set up the underwater camera so they could view the film.

Libby sat forward in her seat on the sofa, watching the sharks as they came on-screen. Her initial encounter with them was identical to the accounts of so many others. The sharks were predatory animals, but there was no sense of imminent danger. Beside her, Chad leaned forward with anticipation as the shadow of the *Bella Siena* came into view.

"It's incredible," Libby said softly, struck once again by the wonder of finding the ship.

"Yes, it is." Chad's voice was heavy with sorrow. "Isabelle should be here to share in this. I should have protected her."

"How could you know?" She touched his shoulder in a gesture of comfort.

"She was so headstrong. Arguing with her never got me anywhere. But I should have stopped her that day when she left. I suspected she might go out on her own, but I didn't even make an attempt."

She could see the guilt eating away at him. "How could you have known she was in danger? Not from sharks, but from someone," Libby said. "You can't blame yourself."

His fingers circled hers, holding on as if her hand was a lifeline. In that moment, Libby forgot everything except a need to offer Chad support in the loss of his friend.

"I wish I could change things," she said.

"Me, too." His other hand reached up to touch her cheek. "But I'm glad you were with me today. I'm glad we shared the discovery together."

Libby leaned slightly into his touch. She'd never expected to feel so close to Chad Watson. He wasn't anything like the image he projected on television. She wanted him to kiss her. She wanted to offer him comfort, but she also needed the haven of his arms, the sense of security he'd given her when they'd escaped the sharks.

As if he read her mind, he leaned closer to her. His lips brushed her cheek. Libby turned her face slightly, so that their lips could connect. It was incredible how much she wanted Chad to kiss her. Two days ago, she'd thought him a handsome—and arrogant—adventurer. Now, though, she knew him as a man who cared about people. For all of the devil-may-care attitude he projected to the public, privately he cared about others.

They'd both shared a rush of emotion, and Libby knew that she wasn't thinking clearly. It didn't matter. For once she decided to put her feelings ahead of her thoughts. She wanted Chad. Even if it was only for an afternoon, she wanted him.

She moved her lips to his, an offering. His first kiss was gentle, tentative. She wanted more. She wanted to give herself to the passion that was rapidly building inside her. She responded to his kiss with hunger. His arms moved around her, pulling her close, as his mouth became more demanding.

The video of the sunken ship was forgotten as Libby allowed Chad to scoop her in his arms. She rested her head against his chest as he carried her into his cabin.

CHAD GENTLY PLACED Libby on the bed. Her almost-dry red curls cascaded over the white pillow, and he lingered over her, touching her hair.

Her arms reached up and pulled him down beside her, as her lips claimed his with a wanton hunger.

Chad had never wanted a woman more. There was something so real about Libby. She was dedicated to her work, yet not hardened. She was strong and soft, beautiful and competent. She was a woman of contradictions. Even as he slowly began to unbutton the cotton blouse she wore, he saw both her passion and shyness. Her green eyes held his gaze as she began to unbutton his shirt.

As his fingers grazed across her nipples, Libby moaned softly and closed her eyes. When he moved down to taste her skin, she tangled her fingers in his hair.

The rays of the afternoon sun slanted through the cabin window, falling like a golden touch across Libby's skin as he finished removing her clothes.

In a few seconds, he was undressed. She held out her arms to him, and he went to her. For an afternoon, the rest of the world was forgotten.

The light had taken on the pale pink tint of dusk, and Libby was resting on his arm. They were both deliciously exhausted.

"You're beautiful," he said. When she started to deny it, he put his finger on her lips.

"You are. The first time I saw you standing on the beach, I wanted to kiss you."

"You roared onto the beach like you were angry."

"I was. With the sheriff."

"I could have taken it personally," Libby said.

He smiled. "I'm glad you didn't."

"I should get ready to leave," Libby said, glancing at the window. "It'll be dark soon." She got up and slipped on her shorts. "I'm surprised Sheriff Darring hasn't been out here looking for me. He was very concerned about me going diving with you."

"I'm sure he was. I hope he does come out to the ship. I need to talk with him. Before you go, let's see the rest of that video. I'll make a copy and you can take it with you. I know you need to study the sharks, and I know you'll keep the discovery of the *Bella Siena* a secret."

Libby's smile was his reward. He trusted her, and he could see how important that was to her.

"I'll get us a glass of wine." He went to the galley, giving Libby time to finish putting on her clothes. He found her in the stateroom, rewinding the tape. Handing her a glass of wine, he set the VCRs to make a copy, then settled on the sofa and pulled her down beside him. She felt just right nestled against his side. There were things he wanted to say to her, but this wasn't the time. It was best just to hold her.

"Ready?" Libby asked as she held up the remote control.

"Go ahead," he said. "We're safe now." He gave her a small squeeze.

Libby hit the play button, then handed the remote to him. The video picked up with a panning shot of the *Bella Siena*. When the first shark swam into view, he felt Libby tense. The shark came at them as if it were on a mission.

Libby remained still and tense until the big creature had swum past. The camera followed it, and she leaned forward.

"Rewind!" she said, her voice strained.

When the film played again, she pointed to the screen. "There! What's that?"

Chad saw it then—a small incision in the shark's head, just behind and above the eye.

"What is that?" Chad paused the film, freezing the frame of the shark's head.

Libby got up and walked to the screen. She traced the thin incision that seemed to be held together with metal surgical staples. "Someone's done something to that shark." She turned to Chad. "But what?"

"I don't know." He pressed the play button and the film continued. "Let's look at the others."

Kneeling on the floor, only inches from the screen, they watched the rest of the tape. They couldn't get a good look at all of the sharks that swam past them, but the ones that were close enough to view all bore similar incisions.

"What's going on?" Libby asked when the video was finished.

"I don't know," Chad answered. "But whatever it is, I don't like it."

"I should contact the sheriff," she answered. "The beaches will have to be closed. If someone is tampering with those sharks, possibly turning them into some kind of attack creature..." She didn't finish.

"Contact Darring *and* the Coast Guard." There was something about Sheriff Darring's buddy-buddy relationship with Barry Klass that troubled Chad. If Libby was going to call in help, she might as well get the Coast Guard, just to be on the safe side. "We need to capture one of those sharks and see if we can figure out what's been done to it."

"I know how to do that," Libby said. "I'll need specific equipment." Her forehead was furrowed with worry. "Chad, the first sharks we saw, the ones that just swam by us just before we found the *Bella Siena.* They were...normal, weren't they?"

He nodded. "They were fine."

"The idea that someone is deliberately doing this—" She broke off.

"Libby," Chad said, going to her and taking her in his arms. He remembered the details surrounding her brother's death. It was a terrible way to lose someone, but it was even worse to contemplate that someone had purposely set up such an event. "I'm so sorry. We'll get to the bottom of this. I promise you."

He felt her take a deep breath, and then straighten in his arms. She was a strong woman. She wasn't a quitter.

"I'd better get into town," she said.

"Let me make a copy of the tape for you to take to Darring. If he gives you any arguments, show it to him."

CHAPTER SIX

LIBBY AIMED the *Quicken* into the waves at an angle. She'd have to adjust her course, but slamming head-on into the swells would take even more time. And time was the enemy.

The bottom of the sun was touching the water to the west, and in a few minutes, it would be dark. The glow of the setting sun made the gulf water an intense aquamarine. Even in her haste, Libby couldn't help but notice the beauty all around her.

She also couldn't stop her mind from going back to memories of Chad. His hands. His lips. The way he held her with such tenderness and desire. Leaving his bed had been one of the hardest things she'd ever done. Yet she was glad she'd forced herself to get up.

After looking at the video, there wasn't a moment to waste. She wasn't simply fighting the natural behavior of the sharks—humans were behind the attacks. And those humans had to be identified and stopped.

She came upon the narrow pass that gave her access to the harbor. Here the tide was treacherous and the channel shallow. Careful navigation was required, and the light was beginning to fail.

Libby negotiated the pass, and in the gentler waters of Charlotte Harbor, she notched the *Quicken* to wide-open.

The sky in the east was already dark, and with stars beginning to twinkle in the dark sky, Libby had to slow. She heaved a sigh of relief when the dock came into view. She felt a little surge of relief when she recognized the tall silhouette of Sheriff Darring. He was standing on the dock as if he were waiting for her.

"Watson radioed me," Darring said as he caught the line Libby tossed him. He tied the *Quicken* to the dock and reached out a hand to help her. "What's going on?"

Libby let him steady her as she jumped from the boat to the dock. She showed the videotape to him. "You won't believe what we caught on film," she said, almost breathless from excitement. "There's something wrong with the sharks. They've been operated on. It could be what's prompting them to attack.''

"No kidding?" Darring reached for the videotape. "You and Watson got that on film?"

"That's right." Libby held the tape against her side. On the ride to the harbor, she'd realized that along with the footage of the sharks, there were shots of the *Bella Siena*. "Sorry, I need this to examine the sharks. I'm going to see if I can determine what portion of their brains have been tampered with."

"I'd like to take a look at it first." Darring reached for the video again.

"We don't have time," Libby said, stepping back. "We need to act now. When this is over, I'll make a copy for you," she suggested, knowing she could edit the tape.

"Fine," Darring said as he took her elbow. His grip was a little too tight and she stepped away from him. "It just makes me a little hesitant to believe these tall tales of surgically altered sharks."

"Look, Sheriff, we need to contact the Coast Guard. I've got to get in touch with some marine biologists in Key West. It's going to be difficult, but we have to catch one of those sharks, and I'll need their help."

"Hold on just a minute. You're saying we need to trap those sharks alive?"

"Yes," Libby said, her words tumbling out in a rush. "If I can figure out what's been done to them—what's making them attack—we can figure out a way to stop them."

"I've got a better idea. Why don't we just use a speargun?" Darring remained standing at the end of the dock. "That'll put an end to the problem immediately."

It was the most expedient solution to the problem, but it wouldn't yield a real answer to the sharks' behavior.

"I think we should hold on to that idea as a last-ditch solution," Libby said evenly. "If we kill the sharks, we may never find out what's been done to them, or why. And we have no idea how many sharks have been altered. Honestly, the smartest approach to this is to capture one shark and give me a chance to examine it."

"I'm not certain we have time for that. What do you suppose has been done to them? Did you get a clear view?'' Darring asked, his voice heavy with worry.

"Clear enough to know someone did something surgical to those sharks." Libby wanted to tug his arm and drag him to a telephone or radio. "You really need to order the beaches closed. Those sharks may do anything."

"Tell me exactly what you saw," Darring insisted. "I can't go off half-cocked. I need to be able to relay the information to the Coast Guard."

"The sharks have been cut just above the left eye. I'm not sure what's done. Maybe some type of transmitter was embedded in the shark's brain. It could be something as simple as a pain stimulus. Or it could be far more complex and sophisticated. Science is capable of many things, not all of them for the betterment of mankind."

"I'm inclined to believe we shouldn't waste our time and effort trapping the sharks. We should destroy them. What good will examining them do?" Darring asked.

"For one thing, once we have a shark to study, we may be able to find out who did this. Whoever managed this advanced surgery must have a facility and a lot of skill. I think we can narrow the field down rapidly, once we have evidence.'' Libby tried to tamp down the frustration she felt. Darring was being deliberately dense.

''I disagree,'' Darring said, moving toward the boats instead of land. ''I'm going out to the *Sea Lady,* and Chad Watson is going to take me to the place where you last saw those sharks.'' Darring boarded the patrol boat as he spoke. He reached down and hefted a speargun. ''I'm putting an end to this, and I have all the tools I need.''

Libby stood on the dock, torn between going with Darring or going to shore to try to get help. ''At least call the Coast Guard. Let's see what kind of help we can get.''

Darring sighed and nodded. ''Okay. I'll radio them from the boat. Hop aboard. We don't have a lot of time to waste. If my gut instincts are correct, we need to get to Chad as fast as we can. He may be in danger.''

''Danger? What kind of danger?'' Libby asked.

''To be honest with you, Dr. Phillips, I've been concerned about Barry Klass ever since he showed up here. But when you told me about those sharks and how they've been changed, it occurred to me that Klass is the only person I know who is capable of what you're suggesting.''

"What do you mean?'' Libby was relieved that the sheriff wasn't immediately pointing the finger of blame at Chad.

"Klass has set up a laboratory in a portion of the abandoned Sea Life exhibit near St. Petersburg. I've heard that along with treasure hunting, he's been working with a lot of marine life. I heard he's training some dolphins and other animals for a Hollywood movie. At first he seemed okay, but he's been asking a lot of questions about Watson and his expedition.''

"You think he may go to the *Sea Lady?*'' Libby was suddenly very afraid for Chad.

"It's a good possibility. He's made several remarks about Chad to me. I let them pass as jealousy. Now I'm not so sure.''

"Call the Coast Guard,'' Libby urged as she climbed aboard his boat.

"I will as soon as we're under way.'' He started the powerful engines. "I know exactly what to do. Don't worry." He turned the boat toward the dark horizon.

CHAD GRIPPED the radio. "Are you sure, Nick?"

"No doubt about it, Chad. Barry Klass isn't a treasure hunter. I don't care what kind of rig he has or how much money. I've spent the past two days checking around like you asked, and nobody has a clue who he is. It's bizarre."

"I suppose he could be a wealthy man who's decided to set himself up in the business." Chad's fingers were clenched around the radio while he talked to his old buddy and diver friend, Nick Corlean, a Miami detective. After what he'd seen with the sharks, he'd wanted to believe that Barry Klass was an interloping fortune hunter. Because if he wasn't, then the chances were very good that he was something a whole lot worse.

"I checked every diving school, every training center. There is no such treasure hunter as Barry Klass. I'll tell you something even stranger. There's no such *person* as Barry Klass."

Chad took a deep breath. "Are you sure?"

"I'm a thorough man. When you said this guy was trying to horn in on your location, I wanted to know more about him. When he didn't show up in any of the usual places, I checked more. And more. And more. The plain fact is, Barry Klass doesn't exist."

"If I had a picture of him, I could scan it and send it to you."

"I'd love to see what he looks like. The freaking invisible man, or so it would seem."

"He's very visible," Chad said. "And he's in Pirate Harbor. Or at least his boat should be docked there." He thought about Libby. "I have to go, Nick. Thanks for looking that up for me."

"Should I fly down there and make myself useful?"

Even though he was worried, Chad couldn't help smiling. "No. At least not yet."

"Anything else I can do for you?"

"There is one thing. We ran across some sharks today. They'd been surgically altered. They'd been cut just behind the eye."

"You're saying they, as if there were dozens of them." Nick's voice was concerned.

"At least a dozen. All of the ones we could see had been cut in the same place."

"That sounds a little ghoulish, Chad."

"It looked a little ghoulish. And the sharks are behaving strangely."

"I'll check into it, see what I can find out, but I have to say, my friend, it sounds more like bad science fiction than fact. You take care," Nick cautioned before he signed off.

Chad was standing up when he heard the sound of a boat motor. He wasn't expecting his crew back, and he hurried on deck to see who was approaching the *Sea Lady*. He recognized the sheriff's patrol boat and turned on a light to help the lawman tie up to the *Sea Lady*. In the glare of the light, he was surprised to see Libby on board. She was as pale as a ghost. He started to ask her what was wrong, but the sheriff began talking.

"Watson, is anyone here?" Darring asked.

"No," Chad said, his focus still on Libby. She looked sick.

"What's all this about sharks being operated on?" Darring asked as he boarded the *Sea Lady*, speargun held lightly in his hand.

"Did Libby show you the tape?" Chad

asked, reaching down to assist Libby. Her eyes were wide. Whether it was fear or shock, he couldn't tell.

"No, she didn't. Actually, I didn't give her time. Why don't we take a look at it now?" Darring glanced down at Libby as Chad pulled her aboard the *Sea Lady*. When she was beside him, he took the tape from her hand.

"Libby, are you okay?" he asked, growing more concerned by the moment at her appearance.

"I was worried about you. Sheriff Darring thought Barry Klass might be out here." She looked over the black gulf waters.

"No time to waste," Darring said abruptly. "We're going to catch one of those sharks, and we're going to figure out how to put an end to all of this madness. The county politicians are already out to have my head because of the loss of revenue from tourists. If I don't make the beaches safe again, I can kiss my job goodbye. Let me see that tape right now."

"What about Klass?" Libby asked.

"What about him?" Darring asked. "We need some evidence before I can go after him."

Libby ran ahead of Chad and blocked the way into the cabin. "Chad, the tape—"

"Is fine," Chad said. He understood Libby's concern and was relieved. She was worried about the location of the *Bella Siena*. "Trust me, it's okay," he said, putting his arm around her shoulders as he set up the VCR and began to play the tape.

Chad fast-forwarded through the tape until they came to the image of a shark. The staples holding the incision together glinted in the camera's light. That shark swam out of the picture only to be replaced by others.

"This is incredible," Darring said, stepping closer to the screen.

The tape went to static, and Chad fast-forwarded it again.

"What's all that blank part?" Darring asked.

"Nothing. We didn't have the camera set properly." Out of the corner of his eye, Chad saw Libby rise from her seat on the sofa, relief clear in her face. But his attention was claimed by Sheriff Darring. The lawman slowly pointed the speargun at the television.

"You found what you were looking for,

didn't you? That's why you blanked out the tape."

"Sorry," Chad said easily. "It was a glitch in my camera work. Nothing as exciting as a treasure find."

"I'm sure," Darring said, "well, I hope you find your damn treasure and take it out of here. Everything around Charlotte Harbor has been in an uproar since you showed up."

More sharks swam across the scene and Darring turned his attention to them. "I see exactly what you're talking about, Dr. Phillips." He turned to Chad, a glint in his eyes. "Let's go take a look down there. Dr. Phillips can stay on the boat in case we need to radio for help."

"The Coast Guard will be here soon," Libby said. "I heard you radio them."

"Yes," the sheriff agreed. "We could wait for them, but I don't think we should."

"The sharks could be anywhere by now," Libby said. "There's nothing to indicate that they remain in the same area. They could be miles from here and not return for several days."

"That's true. Which is why we should act

now. The longer we put it off, the farther away the sharks may get. They could go anywhere. Think of the number of people they can maim or kill."

"What about Klass's facility at St. Petersburg?" Libby asked.

Chad arched his eyebrows. "Klass has a facility on the Florida coast? I haven't been able to track him down at all."

"He wasn't easy to find," Darring said. "I had some old friends in the SEALs. They ran him to ground for me," Darring said. "He's a slippery guy with a dangerous background."

"He was a SEAL?" Libby asked, sitting back on the arm of the sofa.

Chad went and put his arm around her.

"Klass was a SEAL. He was discharged. Dishonorably. He was part of a special unit that was working with sharks as a weapon. He was trying to train them to attack on command. That's why we have to find one of those sharks and prove what he's done to them. And we have to go now, before those creatures are gone." Darring walked to the door. "I can wound the shark with the speargun. Once it's disabled, we can capture it so you can study it, Dr. Phillips.''

"That's not a good plan."

Chad understood that Libby thought hunting for the shark was dangerous, but it was also necessary. "Sheriff, let me speak with Libby for a moment." He took her arm and led her to the galley.

"What's going on?" she asked. "Surely you aren't going to dive tonight?" Her green eyes were wide with fear.

Chad lifted one of her unruly red curls. Gently, he pulled it straight and then let it spring back into a coil. "We won't be gone long, I promise. Darring is right, though, we need to do this now."

"Just say no," Libby begged. "It's too dangerous. Wait for the Coast Guard or some of the crew. Wait until daylight."

His hand moved from her hair to her cheek. "Libby, we'll be fine. That deep in the water, it doesn't matter if it's night or day, you know that. We'll be careful. But we have to try to get one of the sharks. We need evidence to put Klass where he belongs."

Libby closed her eyes and leaned her head

against his palm. It was such a trusting gesture that Chad couldn't help himself. He leaned down and lightly kissed her cheeks. Her passionate response caught him by surprise, and sent an answering surge of desire through him. Libby went from quiet to full-blown passion so quickly. He loved the fact that she didn't govern her feelings for him. She kissed him with complete abandon, and he wanted nothing more than to lift her in his arms and carry her into his cabin. Sheriff Darring and the sharks be damned.

His arms went around her, pulling her against him. He moved his hands down her ribs, following the indention of her waist and the lush swell of her hips. He held her hard against him, knowing that she could feel his desire for her.

"Are you sure you have to go with the sheriff?" Libby asked, her voice slightly roughened.

"I do," he said. He held her shoulders and eased back from her. "I want to get the man who killed Isabelle."

"I'll be waiting for you," Libby promised.

"I'll be back before you even know I'm gone."

CHAPTER SEVEN

CHAD BOARDED the patrol boat after Darring. He was checking the diving gear when the sheriff spoke.

"There's something you should know. Barry Klass is in tight with some of the Coast Guard officers so I didn't call them. I was afraid they'd say something to him."

Chad looked back toward the galley where he'd left Libby near tears. His gut instinct told him not to leave her.

"Where were you diving when you saw the sharks?" Darring asked as he began checking this diving gear.

"About two miles from here. I'll show you." Chad buckled his weight belt on.

"How deep were you?"

"Deep enough that we won't be able to stay down long." He held out a flashlight to the sheriff. "Do you want to hook a light to your belt?"

Darring shook his head. "I'll need both hands to use the speargun. You take the light."

Chad nodded. "Okay. Now we're staying down for twenty minutes. No longer. And you know this is like hunting a needle in a haystack."

"I don't think so," Darring said. "If the sharks are there, they'll find us before we find them."

Chad sat back in the passenger seat and directed the sheriff to a location several miles west of the place where the *Bella Siena* rested. Chad had learned the hard way to trust only a chosen few with the key to a treasure.

"Are you positive this is the place?" Darring asked as he stood in the rocking boat and surveyed the dark horizon.

"We're exactly where we need to be."

"How can you be sure?"

"It's the right place," Chad said, handing the sheriff a pair of goggles. "Let's get this over with. I don't like the idea of Libby being alone on the *Sea Lady*."

Darring laughed. "So, you've developed an

interest in the scientist. I thought you liked flashy women. The good Doctor Phillips seems a little tame for you, Watson. Especially after Isabelle. Now she was a lady with starch in her spine."

Chad couldn't describe the sensation that swept over him. He stopped as he was strapping on his dive tanks. "I didn't realize you knew Isabelle that well."

Darring laughed. "I'd hardly call it well. I met her a time or two in Pirate Harbor. We chatted. She had an opinion on everything."

"Yes, she did." Chad tried to shake off the feeling of uneasiness, but it clung to him. "Sheriff, how did Isabelle really die?"

"What do you mean?" Darring's expression was closed.

"I know you think Isabelle's death wasn't an accident."

"So, Libby's told you about the cuts, has she? And you're wondering why I'd trust myself with a man I considered a potential murderer."

There was no reason to lie. "Yes, and yes. Libby did tell me. And why *are* you diving with me? I didn't kill Isabelle, but why should you believe me?''

Darring picked up the speargun. "I don't trust you, Watson. Not as far as I can throw you. But I trust Klass even less. Still, you have the light and I have the speargun. Now let's get this show on the road." With that, he dropped backwards over the side, the speargun gripped tightly in his right hand.

LIBBY CHECKED her watch, then paced some more. Chad had promised her he'd be back in an hour. He'd caught her in his arms and kissed her, sealing his promise. She closed her eyes and remembered the feel of his lips claiming hers. She'd never experienced such passion. And Chad had assured her he wasn't a liar.

He'd be back in—she checked her watch again—thirty minutes. And he'd left directions showing exactly where he intended to take the sheriff—in the opposite direction from where the *Bella Siena* was located, she noticed. She smiled at the thought. Chad was nobody's fool.

She heard the sound of a boat and nearly tripped running out of the gallery. Chad had obviously been able to talk some sense into Darring. They were already returning.

She ran out on the deck. "Chad!" she called, listening to determine on which side of the *Sea Lady* he was tying up.

There was no answer, and she took a deep breath. It was pitch-black on the deck. The stars were bright, but the moon was just coming up, a waning moon that rose an hour later each night.

"Chad!" She listened intently for an answer. There was only silence.

Slowly she walked to the bow of the ship. "Chad!"

Just as she reached the railing, a man's head popped up. She was so startled, she screamed as she backed up.

"Dr. Phillips, I didn't mean to startle you," Barry Klass said as he climbed on the deck of the *Sea Lady*. "I never suspected you'd be out here." He looked over the boat slowly. "All alone."

"Chad and the sheriff will be back any minute," she said, forcing herself not to panic.

"Where did they go?" Barry's voice was urgent.

The urgency only increased Libby's sense of danger. "They'll be back any minute," she repeated, trying to keep the tremor out of her voice. "I'd like for you to leave."

"Which direction did they go?" Klass pressed. "This is important, Libby. I have to find Darring."

"I don't know. They only said they'd be back soon." She couldn't possibly tell Barry Klass where Chad and the sheriff had gone. She could only assume his intentions weren't noble.

"Libby, this isn't a game. Where are they?"

Barry came toward her so suddenly that she stepped back, tripping on a coil of rope. She felt herself falling. She saw Barry reach for her and the stars spangled across the sky. Then her head struck the deck and there was only blackness.

THE WATER CLOSED over Chad's head. In front of him, the sheriff was swimming with forceful strokes of his flippers. If motion attracted sharks, Darring was going to be successful, Chad thought as he followed him.

When the sheriff turned to him, Chad signaled that they needed to go deeper. The sheriff started down, and Chad was glad he'd thought to have all of the dive suits fitted out with phosphorescent green lines. It was the only way he could tell where Darring was.

He swam up beside the sheriff, swinging the big light in an arc. Fish that had only been pale shadows before took on iridescent colors in the sudden brightness. Chad was once again struck by the beauty beneath the water.

Darring continued swimming, and Chad stayed at his side. They saw the dark shadow of a big fish simultaneously. Chad slowed immediately, making his movements as quiet and small as possible. The sheriff moved past him, headed straight to the fish.

Chad kept the light trained on the shark. It was difficult to tell, but he didn't see any signs of surgery. He'd started toward the sheriff to tell him when the shark changed course and headed right toward Chad. He froze.

The shark was a large one, and it moved like a deadly torpedo, aiming straight at Chad. He swung the light around, hoping to blind the shark, but it didn't work. The creature seemed to pick up speed, its mouth slightly open as it came toward him.

Just when it was within inches, the shark swerved to the right. As it passed, Chad could have reached out and touched it.

Intensely relieved, he turned back to motion to the sheriff that they should head back to the boat. It was enough of a close call, and Darring hadn't even attempted to shoot the shark.

Just as he turned around, he saw Darring lift the speargun. Time froze. Darring was aiming the pointed tip of the deadly spear straight at him.

Chad tried to move, but his body wouldn't respond quickly to any of his commands. The water worked against him so that everything was slow motion. He turned to swim away from Darring, his heart thudding painfully as he found himself facing the shark closing on him fast. Chad was between Darring and the shark. He had to get out of the way.

His arms and legs seemed to flail the water, but his brain was spinning. Now he understood how Darring had been able to find out so much information about Barry Klass when Nick had been unsuccessful. Darring knew because he was either Klass's partner or because the actions he attributed to Klass were actually his own.

Chad dove straight down, but he wasn't quick enough. The point of the spear caught him in the shoulder. It struck with such force that Chad dropped the light. For a moment he felt nothing. He watched the light tumble slowly through the water toward the ocean floor. Then he noticed the cloud of blood that was seeping from the wound.

As he watched the blood paint the water, Chad knew he was in serious trouble. If he didn't bleed to death, the smell of blood would draw more sharks.

CHAPTER EIGHT

LIBBY AWOKE, unsure of where she was. The gentle rocking told her she was on the water, but the cabin was unfamiliar in the darkness. It took several moments for her to remember what had happened. She'd fallen and hit her head on the deck. Now she was in Chad's bed. But where was Chad? And where was Barry Klass? She had no doubts now that Klass was the man who'd killed Isabelle. He'd slipped aboard the *Sea Lady* like a criminal.

Swinging her feet to the floor, Libby eased out of bed. She wasn't certain how long she'd been unconscious. Had Chad returned?

She slipped to the door and gently turned the handle. At first she thought the door was stuck. Pressing down on the handle with all of her weight, she realized it was locked.

CHAD ACCEPTED THE HAND Darring held down to him and allowed the sheriff to drag him into the safety of the patrol boat.

"I expected you to move," Darring said. "I thought you knew the shark had circled and was headed for you. When you saw me point the speargun, I thought you'd get out of the way."

Chad shook his head. He wasn't buying Darring's excuses, but he was in no position to argue. "I'll be okay." He held his hand to the top of his shoulder. Blood was still seeping out, but the flow had slowed. Still, he felt sluggish and sick. "Get me back to the *Sea Lady*."

"I should take you straight to shore, to the hospital," Darring said.

"No. Take me to the *Sea Lady*. Libby can tend the wound."

"It's against my better judgment, but I'll do it," Darring said reluctantly.

In a moment they were speeding across the water, and Chad relaxed. His wound wasn't fatal, but it was debilitating. Which was probably what Darring had been up to all along. But why? He had no doubt that the sheriff had shot him deliberately, but he still couldn't figure out what the lawman's nefarious plan was.

Chad saw the *Sea Lady's* black silhouette

against the starry sky and heaved a soft sigh of relief. He wanted only to see Libby, to make sure she was safe. In an amazingly short time, she'd become very important to him.

As Darring tied the patrol boat to the bigger ship, Chad looked up, expecting to see Libby's face. Surely she'd heard the boat motor. Where was she? His jaw tensed with concern. Something wasn't right.

Darring seemed oblivious to the potential for danger. He boarded the *Sea Lady,* then turned to assist Chad. Once they were on the deck, Chad headed toward the cabin, hoping Libby had simply fallen asleep. The sheriff's hand on his good arm stopped him.

"I wouldn't worry about Dr. Phillips," Darring said. "At least not yet. If you tell me what I want to know, both of you will survive this. She need never know the danger you put her in."

The calculating expression on Darring's face told Chad everything he'd suspected of the sheriff was true. "What is it you want to know?" he asked slowly, hoping now that Libby was asleep.

"Where's the *Bella Siena?*"

"I don't know what you're talking about." He hid the shock he felt at the sheriff's knowledge of the prize he sought. Chad knew once he gave Darring the information he wanted, both he and Libby would be dead.

With a swift and unexpected movement, the sheriff kicked Chad's right leg out from under him. Already weakened by the shoulder wound, he went down hard on the deck.

"I know about the treasure. Why do you think I took a job as sheriff in this godforsaken trap? Nothing here but tourists and retirees," the sheriff said. "I knew about that old ship. Hell, every diver in Florida heard rumors. And I knew if I waited long enough, somebody would come along and find it for me. Now where's the *Bella Siena?*" Darring repeated, his foot on Chad's bad arm. "Tell me and Dr. Phillips won't have to be involved in this."

"Why should I tell you?" Chad asked, refusing to show any of the pain he felt.

"Listen, Watson. What with your reputation and that argument you had with Isabelle at the Yardarm, I've got you perfectly set up to take the fall for Isabelle's murder. I can kill Dr.

Phillips on board your ship, and you'll take the fall for that, too. Now you tell me where the *Bella Siena* is located, and maybe I can make things a little better for you.''

Chad knew that Darring had the upper hand. ''Put Libby on your patrol boat and send her to shore. Tell her anything you want, just get her off the boat. Let me know that she's safe. Then I'll tell you anything you want.''

''You're not exactly in a position to bargain, Watson. For that matter, where is the little lady? I don't want her to miss all the fun.''

LIBBY SLID THE metal ruler into the door lock and gently twisted it. To her satisfaction, she heard the lock mechanism trigger. Easing the door open, she stuck her head out into the narrow hall. There was no sign of Barry Klass.

Moving stealthily, Libby eased up the companionway to the galley. Still, there was no indication anyone else was on board the ship. At last, she made her way to the deck.

Out of the corner of her eye, she caught sight of something moving. As her eyes adjusted to the night, she recognized Klass. He was hiding on the deck—and he had the video camera at eye level. He was filming something.

Returning to the galley, Libby found a meat cleaver. It was a nasty weapon and not as good as a gun, but it would have to do. Returning to the deck, she slowly began to make her way toward Klass.

She was almost at his side when she heard Chad's voice. He spoke with urgency. The voice that answered was Darring. They were back on the *Sea Lady*! But her relief was short-lived.

"Leave Libby out of this," Chad said.

"She's in it, either dead or alive," Darring responded. "If she's more agreeable than Isabelle, maybe she can manage to stay alive. If not..."

"Libby has nothing to do with this."

"The good doctor has seen the sharks. She knows that someone is experimenting with them. She's smarter—and a lot more determined—than I thought. I'm afraid she'll put two and two together."

Libby inhaled sharply. Darring had all but admitted to doing something to the sharks. He was the man behind all of it!

Klass suddenly turned, hearing Libby's

gasp. He showed surprise, then instantly signaled her to stay quiet.

She nodded, then eased closer to him, the meat cleaver behind her back. She'd turned the blade up so that she would hit him with the broad side of it and knock him out.

"Your brother called you Bitsy, and he called you every Saturday morning," Klass said softly. "I was his friend. I'm here to help you."

Libby was stunned. "Who are you?"

"Darring is going to kill Chad. He's after the treasure. You have to trust me." He eased a gun up beside the camera. "If Chad will give him just a little more rope, Darring will hang himself completely. And I'll have it all on tape."

"Who are you?" she repeated, gripping his arm.

"Special agent Barry Case," he said without taking his attention off the camera. "I've been after Darring for months. Now all I want him to do is admit to surgically altering those sharks."

"You knew?" Libby was astounded. "You knew all of this and you didn't stop him?"

"Suspected," Case whispered. "We've examined the sharks. The work on them is interesting."

"Why didn't you do something?"

He held up a hand for silence.

Libby focused on the deck.

"Let Libby go," Chad said.

Darring reached into a duffel bag he'd left by his clothes and pulled out a revolver. "I know Libby knows where the *Bella Siena* is. I can kill you and make her tell me. I can be very persuasive." Darring cocked the pistol and aimed it at Chad.

"I've got to stop him!" Libby could wait no longer. She reached over and pulled the pistol from Barry's hand. Without a second's hesitation, she was running across the deck. "Put the gun down, Darring!" she yelled as she ran.

She heard Barry pounding after her, but she didn't stop. She kept her attention on Darring. The sheriff swung his gun slowly from Chad to her. The expression on Darring's face was pure fury. As his arm straightened to pinpoint his aim, she saw Chad spin on one leg and catch Darring in the knee.

The sheriff went down just as his gun fired.

Libby felt the bullet breeze by her face, only inches away. She was on top of Darring quickly, her gun aimed at his heart. "Drop the gun and put your hands in the air," she said. To her amazement, Darring complied.

Barry ran up behind her and gently took the gun from her hand. She was perfectly willing to let him have it. She dropped to her knees beside Chad. "Are you okay?" she asked, looking around for something to use as a pressure wrap for his wound.

"I'm fine," he said. "And you?"

"A little confused, but otherwise, just fine." She leaned down and kissed his forehead.

"You'll get away with that kind of kiss in front of Klass, but once they're gone, you'll have to do a little better than that."

Libby smiled down at Chad, blinking back the tears. It was great to hear him teasing her. At last she really believed he was going to be okay.

"On your feet," Barry said to Darring, reaching down to pull him up. "You've got a big mouth, and I've got it all on tape."

He pushed Darring toward the radio equipment. "I'll call the Coast Guard now. And a helicopter to fly Chad to the hospital."

Chad accepted Libby's hand as he got to his feet. "No need for that. I'll ride with Libby. I get the feeling she has a lot of things to explain to me, like who you really are."

"Special agent Barry Case. It's a long story and one that Libby should hear. I was in the SEALs with her brother. So was the sheriff here. Libby's brother was working with sharks. The government had the bright idea that if we could train them to attack, they would be tremendous weapons. Unfortunately, after her brother and several other SEALs were accidentally killed, the government abandoned the project. Somehow, Darring got hold of the experiments and he's been conducting his own research, haven't you, Sheriff?"

"I have nothing to say to you," Darring said.

"You really knew my brother?" Libby asked. "Was he deliberately killed while training sharks?"

"It was an accident," Barry emphasized. "He'd volunteered to work with the sharks, but he wouldn't go along with the experiments.

He insisted they could be trained like dolphins. He was doing what he loved, Libby.''

She looked at Darring. ''What did you do to those sharks? How did you make them attack people?''

''I didn't get them to attack anyone,'' the sheriff retorted. ''You can't lay that on me. I simply put in a radio transmitter so I could track them. I've done nothing to change their nature.''

Libby wasn't sure she believed him, but it wouldn't take long until she had it figured out. ''I intend to examine the sharks, and you better hope that's what I discover,'' Libby told him as Barry led him away to make the call to the Coast Guard.

EPILOGUE

LIBBY APPLIED the salve to the wound on Chad's shoulder. It had almost healed. In the past several weeks, they'd both spent a lot of time telling each other about their pasts and letting old wounds mend.

"We should bring the chest up today," Chad said, eagerness clear in his voice. "Raising the ship will take a bit longer."

Libby smiled at him. "I can't wait to see what's in it." Waiting for his wound to heal had almost killed Chad. At last, though, he'd been able to lead his dive team on the recovery of the treasure. Soon they'd know what the large chest they'd found in the *Bella Siena* contained.

He pulled her close. She let her body mold to his, wondering again at the surge of emotion that flooded through her at Chad's slightest touch. She'd fallen deeply in love with him.

"I spoke with Barry this morning," she said, pushing her red curls out of her eyes as she looked up at Chad. "We got the last of the sharks. We've removed the transmitters that Darring implanted, but the sharks will be kept for observation."

"The radio transmitters were really used to track the sharks?" Chad asked.

"So it would seem. But I know that's not what Darring was really up to, and I don't think he's going to admit to anything."

"Why did the sharks attack the swimmers?" Chad asked, his hand gently moving up and down her arm.

"I can't say for certain. As the waters become more and more populated, there'll be more shark attacks. My biggest concern was the idea that the sharks had moved into brackish water. But Darring confessed that he dumped Isabelle's body in the harbor water after she was dead. He said he only meant to frighten her, but she'd bled to death. Then he thought to blame her death on the sharks, but the coroner's examination put him in a spot."

"Poor Isabelle," Chad said. "She found the ship and she paid with her life."

She felt the sudden tension in him and knew that he had still not recovered from the death of his friend and partner. No matter what price Darring paid in the justice system, it would never be high enough for Chad.

"It also turns out the research facility in St. Petersburg we thought was Barry's actually belonged to Darring. We believe all of the sharks involved were raised in captivity. It's a horrible thought, isn't it, that someone could teach them to attack as a unit."

"I hope Darring never sees the free world again."

Libby reached up and touched Chad's jaw, letting her fingers slid to his lips. "I'm sorry, Chad. I wish I could change things."

He kissed the tips of her fingers. "You can."

"How?" she asked.

"When this is over, will you stay on with me?"

The question came out of nowhere, but it was something Libby had given a lot of thought to in the past three weeks. She'd tried to view this time with Chad as a magical adventure. She'd done everything she could not to think about the future. Once he finished his quest for treasure, she'd understood that he would leave. But deep in her heart, she'd fantasized about a future with Chad. It was just something they hadn't spoken about. There had been too many other things going on.

"Stay with you?" she asked, hoping he couldn't hear the sudden acceleration in her heartbeat. "You mean as a team member? I hardly think you need a marine scientist."

Chad touched her chin, lifting her face so that she had to look at him. "I mean as my wife," he said slowly. "It was a poor proposal." He sank to one knee. "Let me try again. Libby, will you marry me?"

She couldn't stop the smile. "Yes," she said. "Yes, I will."

Chad stood up, pulling her into his arms and kissing her. "I think we should celebrate," he said, his lips moving possessively down to her neck. "I know exactly how we should go about it."

"Sounds like a—"

Libby was interrupted by the clearing of a throat. She turned in Chad's arms to find a crew member, Reginald, standing behind her.

"Bad timing," he admitted with a wry grin. "Sorry to interrupt, but we got the webbing on the chest. We're pulling it up right now."

"Thanks," Chad said. "I'll be right with you."

Libby leaned to whisper in his ear. "I know how long you've waited for this. Let's see what treasures the ocean holds." She took his hand and together they walked to the bow of the ship where the large winch was pulling up cable.

The chest broke the water, and Chad's crew swung it over the deck before lowering it down.

Libby couldn't help the excitement that shot through her as Chad went forward and carefully began loosening the metal bands that held the trunk shut. After a moment, Reginald helped him lift the lid.

The sunlight caught the glint of gold as a loud sound of approval went up from the crew. Libby was stunned by the jewels. Rubies, emeralds and sapphires sparkled in the light, even after hundreds of years in seawater.

Chad stepped back so that he stood beside her. He took her hand and looked at his crew.

One of them handed out glasses and another began popping the corks on champagne bottles. They all turned to Chad.

"To great treasure," Chad said. "Gold, jewels and the love of a good woman." He turned to Libby and kissed her. "I'd like to introduce you to my fiancée."

A cheer broke out from the crew, and Libby forgot everything except Chad as he circled his arms around her and began to kiss her.

Two women fighting for their lives...
and for the men they love...

INTIMATE DANGER

Containing two full-length novels of enticing
romantic suspense from top authors

Susan Mallery
Rebecca York

Look for it in September 2002—wherever books are sold.

More fabulous reading from
the Queen of Sizzle!

LORI FOSTER

with

Forever
and Always

Back by popular demand are the scintillating stories of
Gabe and Jordan Buckhorn. They're gorgeous, sexy
and single...at least for now!

Available wherever books are sold—September 2002.

And look for Lori's *brand-new* single title,
CASEY in early 2003

HARLEQUIN®
Makes any time special ®

HARLEQUIN®
INTRIGUE®

brings you an exciting
new 3-in-1 collection
from three of your favorite authors.

Gypsy Magic

by

REBECCA YORK,
ANN VOSS PETERSON
and PATRICIA ROSEMOOR

Ten years ago, scandal rocked small-town
Les Baux, Louisiana: the mayor's wife was murdered,
her Gypsy lover convicted of the crime.
With her son sentenced to death, the Gypsy's
mother cursed the sons of the three people
who wrongly accused him.

For Wyatt, justice is blind.

For Garner, love is death.

For Andrei, the law is impotent.

Now these men are in a race against time to find the real
killer, before death revisits the bayou. And only true love
will break the evil spell they are under....

*Available OCTOBER 2002
at your favorite retail outlet.*

HARLEQUIN®
Makes any time special ®